MALLAIG ROAD

MALLAIG ROAD

A Journey Through Childhood

The Early Life of Alexander Maclean

A Novel

ROBERT DEWAR

Matador
Unit E2 Airfield Business Park,
Harrison Road, Market Harborough,
Leicestershire. LE16 7UL
Tel: 0116 2792299
Email: books@troubador.co.uk
Web: www.troubador.co.uk/matador
Twitter: @matadorbooks

ISBN 978 1803130 965

British Library Cataloguing in Publication Data.
A catalogue record for this book is available from the British Library.

Typeset in 11.5pt Adobe Garamond Pro by Troubador Publishing Ltd, Leicester, UK

Matador is an imprint of Troubador Publishing Ltd

In loving memory of my Parents, Douglas and Sally Dewar

For an account of Alexander Maclean's
later years, read *Hemispheres*.

The childhood shows the man,
As morning shows the day.

Paradise Regained
John Milton

Chapter One

On the 20th April of 1965, soon after Easter, Alexander's family moved into the small brick built house on Mallaig Road, on the eastern fringes of Rondebosch, a comfortable, middle class Cape Town suburb. The house, while not being foursquare exactly, was a determined oblong (with a small live-in servant's annexe behind the garage to one side of the house, across from the kitchen). It crouched beneath a single span of red tiled roof with a gable at either end, and there was a covered veranda, or *stoep*, at the top right corner, and the house's forthright appearance seemed to Alexander to hold the promise of stability and permanence.

Stability and permanence were qualities whose recent absence in his life the ten year old Alexander could not consciously have communicated, but he craved them even so. Only one and a half months earlier, he and his family had been living in a large house built of stone, set in an acre of landscaped garden in Nairobi, and since that time there had been the long journey by train to the coast with his mother and brother (while his father drove the car down), and a stay with Alexander's maternal grandparents at their home in Mombasa, and then the wonders and delights of the voyage by sea down the East African coast (calling at Dar es Salaam, Beira, Lourenço Marques, Durban, Port Elizabeth, and finally, Cape Town). The family had spent one and a half weeks at a hotel in Sea Point, a suburb overlooking the Atlantic Ocean, round the corner from Cape Town city centre, while Alexander's parents had searched for a house to buy. And this sensible house with three bedrooms, set in a modest but respectable neighbourhood, was the house they had chosen.

'Hey – Sandy!' Alexander's brother, Roy, yelled in the garden as the removals men unloaded the van and hauled furniture and boxes into the house. 'What do you think lies through those bushes at the bottom of the garden?'

'Let's go see!'

The two brothers, Roy, the youngest by one and a half years, as skinny and tanned and blonde headed as his older brother, both wearing shorts, and socks which had slipped down towards their ankles, ran down the side of the house towards the wire mesh fence at the bottom of the garden. They clambered over the fence, and were almost immediately lost from sight amidst the dense undergrowth. But they barged their way through it for a distance of about fifteen yards, and suddenly they came across a stream flowing between steep banks covered in plant growth.

'A river!' Alexander exclaimed. 'We must build a boat.'

'Yeah – we'll build a boat!'

The boys scrambled down to the water's edge. The river was barely a river: it was only about fifteen feet broad at this point, but the water was clear, and water grasses grew along the edges of the stream. A pair of coots could be seen a little way upstream. The brothers stood staring at the water for a while, and Alexander asked 'I wonder what lies beyond the river?'

'Can we get across?' Roy asked.

'We'd better not do that right now. Mum will wonder where we've got to. But we'll go exploring soon.'

'Alright, maybe we could build a raft; it'll be easier than building a boat,' Roy said.

'And we can make a camp in these bushes,' Alexander responded.

The brothers pushed through the undergrowth again, which consisted for the most part of slim, closely spaced single-stemmed saplings between four feet and six feet tall, from whose stems broad leaves, dark on top and pale on their undersides, grew directly, and they clambered back over the fence at the bottom of the garden. No one had missed them.

Alexander and his brother Roy had both been born in Nairobi. Their father, also named Alexander, had been born in Mombasa, and their mother in Nakuru, a small town in Kenya's Rift Valley. Alexander's paternal grandfather, Rory, had been an engineer with the colony's Public Works Department. When Rory's son left the army in 1945 he was a good looking, cheerful, uncomplicated, gregarious young man with flaming red hair and deep blue eyes, his Scottish descent clearly apparent. He was as conventional and thoroughly decent as most young men of that period in the colony; he had enjoyed his army service tremendously, and he would have remained in the army and made it his career had his parents permitted him. Instead, they had sent him to university in England, where he had graduated as a mechanical engineer.

Olivia Copeland's father was English. Her mother was an American, born in France. Like the Macleans, they had arrived in the colony soon after the Great War. Olivia's father had been owner and manager of a small hotel on the Kenya coast, not far from Mombasa, when Alexander Maclean had stayed there for a fortnight's holiday, after returning from university in England in late 1951. The two young people had immediately fallen in love, and Alexander Maclean had married Olivia in Mombasa Cathedral in late 1952.

Olivia was a quiet, not very sociable young woman, artistic, creative and well read, and given to occasional moodiness. She was also rather pretty, with dark brown hair and the same thoughtful grey eyes that her son Alexander was to inherit. It was from her that Alexander gained his love of books and reading, and perhaps his skills with drawing. From his father he gained a love of music, and a quality that only really became pronounced some years after he had left school: a capacity for being liked, and an easy way with people.

Alexander's paternal grandparents had both been born in Scotland. They had left Kenya in 1963, along with Alexander's father's two younger sisters and their families, a few months before *Uhuru* (Kenyan independence), and had settled in Cape Town. Now, less than two years later, Alexander's father had also brought his family to South Africa. The Maclean clan was united once again. Alexander's father had been working for an American oil company in Nairobi, and he had been offered a job at the company's Cape Town offices. Alexander's grandfather, Rory, was now working as an engineer for the Cape Town Municipality.

For some years Alexander was to remember the family's life in Kenya as a Paradise lost. He could recall no unhappy times in Kenya, and he remembered a comfortable, expansive living beneath a sun which always shone, a lifestyle which his family was unable to duplicate to a similar extent in South Africa. It was easier for Roy. Roy's memories of life in Kenya went back only three, or at the most, three and a half years. Alexander's memories of Kenya however went back at least five years; longer than that in some instances. But Alexander was to grow to love Cape Town, and decades later, he would remember Cape Town and the Cape Peninsula with nostalgia, even though those years had not been entirely free of pain, heartache and loss.

Opposite the house the Macleans moved into on Mallaig Road was a vacant plot of land, and this permitted a fine view of the Newlands face of Table Mountain from the sitting room window.

Alexander would gaze often at that mountain. Its moods changed with the seasons. In the summertime the dominant mood was one of serenity; in the wintertime, the mountain sometimes seemed angry. What would he find if he could ever reach the top?

On either side of this vacant plot were houses similar in size to the Macleans' house; both had young families living in them. There were many young families in the neighbourhood. There were two little girls living in the house to the left of the vacant plot of land. Roy was to have more to do with them over time than his older brother was. Living in the house to the right of this empty plot was a boy about Alexander's own age, and his baby sister. Alexander and Roy were to meet the boy later during that first day at their new home.

At about noon, Alexander's mother called the boys over. 'You've got to have something to eat and drink,' she told them. 'I've made some sandwiches and some Ribena. You can have them on the lawn.'

The house was newly built. There were as yet no trees to sit beneath, and the sun was warm, but the brothers were accustomed to the far stronger equatorial sun of Kenya, and they did not mind sitting cross-legged on the lawn. Their mother had made cheese sandwiches with brown bread. Both boys were picky eaters, but they did not mind cheese. They had barely finished their meal, and gulped down their Ribena, when Roy exclaimed 'Look! Our bikes!'

The removals men had brought the boys' bicycles from the van and leaned them against the wall of the stoep. Alexander and Roy made a beeline for their bicycles.

'Mum!' Alexander yelled. 'Can we go for a ride?'

Their harassed mother turned and saw her sons' beaming faces. 'Alright. But don't go far. And don't stay out for long. Have you got that, Sandy?'

'Alright Mum. We wont go far,' Alexander replied. 'Come on then!' he said to his brother.

The brothers wheeled their bicycles through the garden gate.

Alexander felt the tyre pressures between fingers and thumb. The tyres needed air. He leaned his bicycle against the low garden wall and unclipped the bicycle pump from the bike's frame, and began to pump up the tyres. Roy did likewise. They saw a boy in short trousers and sandals standing on the opposite pavement, watching them. A nondescript, shaggy-haired dog was sitting alongside him. It was a Tuesday, but school was out for the Easter holidays. Alexander pushed off on his bike and headed diagonally across the street, then leaned to one side and extended a foot to support himself.

'Hullo,' he said. The dog came and sniffed his bare leg. Alexander leant down and patted the top of its head. The dog stuck out its tongue and panted, and rolled its eyes up towards him.

'Hullo,' the boy replied, smiling. 'Where are you from?'

'Kenya. We came by sea.'

'That's a nice bike.'

'Thanks. What's your name? Mine's Sandy.'

'Stewart. What standard are you in?'

'Standard?'

'At school!'

'I don't know,' Alexander responded. 'I was in form three in Nairobi.'

'How old are you?' Stewart asked.

'Ten.'

'So am I. Then you'll probably be in standard three, like me.'

Alexander smiled. 'That'll be nice. Perhaps we'll be in the same class. Have you seen the river below our house?'

'Yeah. I wish I had a boat.'

'So do I!' Alexander exclaimed. 'My brother and I will build one, a raft maybe. You can help.'

Stewart, who had short dark hair and green eyes, and was tanned even darker than the two Maclean boys, smiled again. Alexander liked his smile.

'I'd like that,' Stewart said. 'I used to be able to reach the river easily, then they built your house. Now I have to go to the end of the road to reach the river.'

'You can visit us,' Roy said, 'and we can go play at the river together.'

'OK,' Stewart responded.

'We're going for a ride,' Alexander said. 'Have you got a bike?'

'Yeah. Let me go fetch it. We'll go for a ride together. I can show you around.'

Stewart disappeared into the garage at the side of the house, and reappeared with a rather battered bicycle. 'Let's go!' he said.

The three boys headed around the corner into Golden Grove Road, Stewart in the lead, all three pedalling hard up the slight uphill which ran alongside the school's playing fields. This was Kromboom Park Primary School, and it was where the brothers would be going to school, beginning what would be the second term of the Cape school year, starting in just under a week's time.

Alexander was thinking 'I'll have a friend at school now.'

The early autumn weather continued fine for the remainder of that week, and during the following weekend also. The air in the early mornings and in the evenings had a slight chill to it. In the evenings, smoke rose from some of the chimneys of neighbouring houses. The brothers' parents were both at home during this time. Their father would not be starting work until the following Monday. He went around the house inside, touching up scratches and removing marks left by the builders. He revarnished all the wooden window frames outside, and the front door and garage doors also. Roy, who loved working on things, helped their father, but Alexander's involvement was less enthusiastic, driven more by a sense of duty. Their mother turned the new house rapidly into a home. Soon there were familiar oil paintings hanging on the walls, and much loved ornaments on the mantelpiece above the fireplace, and on top of the built-in bookshelves to either side of the fireplace.

The family visited a garden centre, and came away with a six foot tall American plane tree sapling, which they planted on the front lawn. This was a fast growing tree, and it was hoped that it would in time provide shade. Alexander's mother had also bought a variety of shrubs, mostly perennials, which she dug into the garden, which had consisted of nothing but lawn when they moved in.

The Macleans had brought their two-tone red and black Vauxhall Velox car with them by sea. Standing on the quayside at Mombasa, Alexander, his brother, and their parents had watched their family car being raised high into the air above them on a wooden palette by a big harbour crane, and then lowered into one of the ship's holds. Alexander's father now gave the car a thorough cleaning, removing the grease which had been liberally applied to the bodywork against the salt sea air.

A middle aged Cape Coloured man appeared on Thursday morning, while Mrs. Maclean was working in the garden. '*Merrem*, good morning *Merrem*,' he greeted her. 'I am a gardener. I can look after your garden.'

Mr. Maclean joined his wife outside, and greeted the man. Then he turned to his wife.

'Perhaps he could come once a week, to do the mowing and digging and weeding?' he asked her.

'You and I can do that, darling.'

'I know, but it would be nice if you did n't have to.' He turned to the man. 'How much will you charge once a week for a full day? You can do some digging, and tackle the weeds, and mow the lawn.'

'*Ja Baas*, I can do that. For a full day you can give me three Rand. I can come on Fridays.'

'Will you be here tomorrow?'

'*Ja Baas*. At eight o'clock.'

A number of neighbours came across to introduce themselves over the next few days. Alexander's father, sociable as always, enjoyed their visits. These visitors would be ushered indoors, and served tea or coffee, and shop-bought biscuits. Olivia Maclean was far less of an extrovert than was her husband, but she was grateful for the sense of neighbourhood community that she discerned. Stewart's mother, Mrs. Fleming, took pains to inform Olivia Maclean that her husband was an architect, and that he had designed their home. Her accent was a touch affected, taking care not to flatten the South African vowel sounds. Alexander's mother spoke the English of the Kenya settler class, which to the South African ear sounded like an upper class English accent from the British Isles.

Stewart's home was not as boxlike and uniform as some of the others in the street. It had a steeply pitched roof of shingles for a start, instead of the ubiquitous red factory-made tiles, and each gable had a small window in it. In places the walls were faced with dressed stone. The chimney, which reached high above the roof, was also finished in stone. The house was only a few years old. The houses to the right of Golden Grove Road as it went up the hill were older than those where the Macleans now lived. The former had been built in the late forties and the early fifties. They had fairly large trees in their gardens, and well established garden hedges. The houses in Mallaig Road to the left of the junction with Golden Grove Road, including the Macleans' house, had been built very much more recently. In some cases, as with the vacant plot in front of the Maclean home, there was still room for building.

To their right, the Macleans' neighbours were a retired couple, the Arbuthnotts; to their left, an Italian immigrant family with a very attractive daughter aged about thirteen. She was as leggy as a colt, with a wide mouth which smiled easily, and long shining hair as dark as a raven's wing. She greeted the Maclean brothers over the wire mesh fence on the afternoon of their first day, with only the faintest (and rather attractive) trace of Italian in her accent, and within minutes, they were both charmed by her; indeed, Roy fell straight away in love with her. Her name was Paola.

Stewart's mother told Mrs. Maclean that she knew of a good, reliable maid who was available to work for the Macleans. The family she had been working for had recently been transferred to Johannesburg. Alexander's mother met this woman on Friday afternoon. The Cape Coloured woman was middle aged, short and stout, with features that smiled easily. Her name was Dorcas. It was soon clear that she was fond of children, and both the brothers were soon to take to her.

'Can you start work next Tuesday?' Mrs. Maclean asked the woman.

'Yes *Merrem*.'

Dorcas would come to work for Mrs. Maclean five and a half days a week. She would not be living in: her home was in the Cape Coloured neighbourhood of Crawford, which lay across the veld beyond the far side of the Kromboom River as it ran below the Macleans' house. It was an easy walk from her home across the *veld* and over the river further along from the Macleans' house, where there was a ford with closely spaced flat topped rocks across the river. If in the wintertime the ford was inundated, there was the Kromboom Road Bridge she could use, which stood not far to the north of Mallaig Road. Dorcas was willing and amiable, and in time she would come to earn the Maclean family's affection and respect.

Chapter Two

On Friday morning, leaving Joseph, the new gardener, at work in the garden, the boys' father drove his family to Rondebosch Station, where Olivia Maclean and her sons were to take the commuter train into Cape Town. Mr. Maclean would collect his family at the station around lunchtime. The journey into Cape Town took about twenty-five minutes, with brief halts at Rosebank, Mowbray, Salt River and Woodstock. Alexander could smell the electricity in the air as the train, which fed off an overhead electric cable, pulled in alongside the platform. He was tremendously excited, and could barely keep still on the wide bench seat upholstered in heavy duty faux blue leather. His mother sat on the bench seat opposite her sons. Alexander enjoyed train travel almost as much as he enjoyed sea voyages. Roy however was anxious.

'Are there toilets on the train?' Roy asked his mother. 'What happens if I need to go to the toilet?'

'We'll be at Cape Town Station in twenty minutes,' his mother told him. 'You can use the lavatory there if you need it.'

Cape Town Station, a modern, light-filled concourse, impressed Alexander. Already, he had an eye for architectural design. He had to stop to admire the ancient steam locomotive that was mounted in the centre of the concourse. By the age of ten, Alexander knew that he was keen on ships and boats, trains, and interesting buildings – interests which were to remain with him all his life. As they exited the station building, they looked up Adderley Street, towards Table Mountain, which was framed by Devil's Peak to the left and Lion's Head to the right.

'Gosh!' Alexander declared. 'Look how high it is!'

The mountain, like some vast and ancient protective deity, sheltered the city in its secure embrace. Its bulk and height terminated in a flat table-top, with a tiny pimple on the extreme right hand side of the table. This was the top cable station. The lower slopes of the mountain descended to the old established suburbs of Gardens and Oranjezicht. On the lower slopes of Devil's Peak was grassland with groups of scattered pine trees. The upper part of the mountain was sheer rock, rising vertically to the flat top. The characteristic flat cloud cover of summer was absent, for in the still, early autumn weather, the atmospheric conditions were inopportune.

At Stuttafords, one of Cape Town's two big department stores, the boys and their mother took a moving escalator upstairs. Alexander, who had never seen a moving escalator before, was extremely dubious. He hesitated at its foot, watching the unforgiving serrated steel segments emerge from beneath the sharp teeth at the bottom of the escalator.

'Come on!' Roy called him, having jumped straight onto the moving stairs. Roy was always at home with mechanical devices. Alexander screwed up his courage and jumped, clutching at the rubberised hand grip as it moved alongside. 'It's easy – see?' Roy said.

There was a department specialising in school uniforms. The brothers needed to be kitted out for their new school. Their mother bought them two pairs of grey shorts each, and two pairs of grey flannels for winter wear (the shorts and flannels both a size larger than needed right now, whose waists Mrs. Maclean would take in, and whose legs she would take up, and which she could let out again as the boys grew), a snake buckled belt each, seven pairs of knee length grey socks, and seven pairs of short grey socks, four pairs of short sleeved and four pairs of long sleeved white shirts each, a tie each (with a spare tie between the two of them against accidents), two green sweaters each, a blazer each in the school colours of narrow vertical stripes of green and orange (the blazers rather large in each case, so that the brothers had room to grow into them, for blazers were expensive), and a school cap each, also in striped green and orange, with one spare cap between the two of them. The boys already had school satchels of brown leather, and black school shoes.

'And what about their PT kit, Madam?' asked the middle aged lady who was serving them.

'Oh – I had forgotten that,' Mrs. Maclean said. 'What will the boys need?'

'At Kromboom Primary they wear white gym shorts, sleeveless white vests, and long sleeved green tops in the winter, short white socks, and white gym shoes, Madam,' the shop assistant answered her.

'Very well. I will take a pair of gym shorts each, but a size smaller than the school shorts I've bought, two sleeveless white vests each, and a pair of long sleeved tops each. My sons already have tennis plimsolls which will do for gym also'

Children's clothing was found on the same floor. Mrs. Maclean bought the brothers some new underwear. That done, she treated her sons afterwards to ice creams in the store's cafeteria. Mrs. Maclean was shocked at how much money she had spent. She ordered herself a pot of tea and a slice of sponge cake. She looked at her sons. 'Dont grow too fast,' she told them. The brothers grinned.

'Can we take the cable car to the top of the mountain?' Alexander asked. His father had told him about the cable car which took visitors to the very top of the mountain.

'Not this time, Sandy,' his mother replied. 'We have n't got time. But we will, one weekend.'

The following Monday, the 26th April, Mrs. Maclean drove her husband to Rondebosch Station, leaving the house at half past seven in the morning. Her husband would take the Peninsula commuter line into Cape Town. It was his first day at his new job. At the station Mrs. Maclean did not get out of the car, but kissed her husband as he sat on the wide bench seat alongside her. 'Are you nervous, Alex?' she asked.

Alexander Maclean laughed. 'I feel like a new boy going to school for the first time.'

'It 'll be alright, you 'll see. Good luck darling.'

Alexander Maclean got out of the car, his briefcase in one hand, and as he was about to disappear from sight he turned and waved at his wife, who smiled and waved back, then turned the car around and headed for home. Once the boys had begun school, it would be a challenge to get both her husband and her sons off in time. Perhaps she could arrange that Dorcas arrived a little early. The boys would have to set off for school before she had returned from the station. But today they had an appointment at the school at ten o' clock. At quarter to ten, wearing shorts and shirts which were clean and pressed, and shoes which the brothers had been made to polish that morning, their faces scrubbed and their straight blonde hair neatly combed, Alexander and his brother accompanied their mother on foot up Golden Grove Road and around the corner into Stuart Road. A short distance along was the entrance to the school. They were to meet the headmaster. Alexander felt somewhat anxious. He knew that this was an important occasion, for his mother had warned both boys to be on their best behaviour.

The Head, Mr. Powell, kept them waiting for about ten minutes. The boys sat stiffly on uncomfortable straight backed chairs, and watched the young woman at a desk across from them as she typed. Then her intercom buzzed, and she looked up and smiled at Mrs. Maclean. 'The Headmaster will see you and your sons now.'

Mr. Powell was in his forties. He was dressed in a dark jacket and grey slacks. He wore a rather bright green tie. His hair was slicked back from a high forehead, and he peered at the boys from above reading glasses. Smiling at the brothers, he asked them, 'Are you looking forward to starting school with us?'

Roy wriggled in his seat. Alexander felt it was incumbent upon him to answer, so he replied 'Yes.' His mother nudged him. 'Yes Sir.'

'That's good.' Mr. Powell turned to Mrs. Maclean. 'How many years of schooling had your sons completed in … in Kenya, I believe?'

'Roy, the youngest, was in form two, so it was his fourth year at primary school. But both my sons were at nursery school before starting primary school. Alexander was in form three, his fifth year.'

'Are your sons academically minded, Mrs. Maclean, or do they prefer sports?'

'Well … Roy is probably a little more interested in sports than his brother. Alexander is prone to asthma, and he reads a lot. But they both get out and about a great deal. I would n't call Alexander a swot.'

Mr. Powell laughed. 'The happy medium, eh? We encourage our children to participate in sports, but not to the exclusion of academic achievement.' Looking at the brothers, he continued 'Perhaps not rugby, but football? Of course, in the summer, the boys play cricket.'

Alexander was not sure he was very keen on football. Or cricket. At Lavington, his school in Nairobi, he had played tennis.

Mr. Powell peered over his spectacles at Mrs. Maclean. 'We have an excellent choir. Do either of your sons show promise in that direction?'

'Alexander sang in the school choir in Nairobi. He enjoyed it very much – did n't you?' Alexander's mother said, looking at him.

'Yes,' he replied. In fact, he rather liked the idea of joining the school choir here.

'We'll be happy to offer your sons a place each. Roy can start off in standard two, and Alexander in standard three. There's some paperwork to be completed. Miss van Rensburg outside will show you. Have your sons got school uniforms yet?'

'Yes, Mr. Powell, I took the boys to town last week.'

'Excellent. We begin our school day at eight o' clock, with assembly in the hall. Can your sons report to the office tomorrow morning at a quarter to eight?'

'Thank you. I shall make sure they're here tomorrow on time.'

Alexander was not looking forward to tomorrow morning. On the way back home, his mother said to her sons 'It will be nice – you'll see. You will soon be looking forward to school each day.'

Alexander was not sure of that. Nor was his brother. It was a subdued pair of little boys who took a Dinky Toy car each onto the lawn when they got home. They knelt on the grass, and played in near silence for a while.

'I wish we had n't left Nairobi,' Alexander said after a while.

'Me too.'

Stewart Fleming was a good looking, popular boy. He had a ready smile, and a way with him which predisposed people to like him, and which encouraged teachers – in fact, adults in general – always to give him the benefit of the doubt. He had a generous heart. When he saw the two Maclean brothers being led into assembly by Miss van Rensburg on Tuesday morning (Alexander feeling as if absolutely everyone in the hall was staring at him), he grinned at Alexander, who was shown a place at the end of the row that Stewart was sitting in. Alexander smiled rather shakily back at him. When the opening chords of the South African national anthem – *Die Stem* – were played on the piano, Alexander did not recognise the tune, and he stood up again a few seconds later than everyone else. Nor did he know the words to the national anthem. But he would learn them very quickly, and before long, he would sing as enthusiastically as anyone else, in his clear, high treble.

The Headmaster and the teaching staff, standing in an orderly row on the stage up front, bowed their heads after the first verse of the national anthem had been sung, and Alexander joined in singing the Lord's Prayer. The tune was familiar to him. Then everyone but the Headmaster sat down. He spoke for a while, but Alexander paid him little attention. At assembly's end, the school song was sung. Alexander did not of course know the words, but he was soon to pick them up.

He was not looking forward to the day.

However, during first break, Stewart sought him out, and made him feel welcome. Not far away, Alexander could see his brother with another group of smaller boys. The morning passed, and almost before Alexander realised, it was time to go home. He found his cap in his satchel, and put it on. It had been impressed upon him by Stewart that he was always to wear his school cap when out in public. Within a few minutes Roy, who had been laughing with another boy, joined him, and they covered the few minutes' walk home.

At home, the boys' mother kissed them both on the cheek. 'Well – I see you are both alive. How did it go?'

'It was alright,' Roy replied.

'Yeah – it was n't bad,' Alexander added.

'Have you got homework?'

'Some,' Alexander said.

'And what about you, Roy?'

'I have to do some sums,' her youngest son answered.

'Make sure you've done your homework by suppertime, both of you.'

'Alright Mum,' both brothers answered.

Dorcas, the new maid, was working in the kitchen. She and Mrs. Maclean had gone shopping that morning at Chong's, the Chinese owned grocers and general dealers nearby. Dorcas had baked some chocolate chip biscuits. These (together with peanut cookies) were to prove, over time, to be specialities of hers, which pleased the brothers. Dorcas gave the boys two each, which brought a shy thank you from each brother. They had barely seen Dorcas arrive for her first day's work at the Maclean home before they had had to leave for school. It would take them a little while to feel completely at ease in her company.

'Would you like some cold orange juice?' Dorcas asked the boys.

The boys gulped down their cold drinks.

'Stewart has a dog. Can we get a dog?' Alexander asked his mother, as she entered the kitchen to ask Dorcas to make her some coffee.

'I don't think we'll get a dog, Sandy,' Mrs. Maclean replied, smiling fondly at her eldest son. 'But we can get a cat. A Siamese cat if we can find one for sale.'

'Oh yay! I bet we'll be the only house in the street with a Siamese cat!'

The boys had known and admired a Siamese cat which had belonged to family friends in Nairobi. They had been impressed by its raucous voice, and by its engaging, friendly manner. It had behaved more like a dog than a cat. Alexander hoped they would not have long to wait before they had just such a cat of their own.

On Saturday morning the brothers and their parents drove to Muizenberg, a township on False Bay, which they reached via the rather narrow and winding Main Road as it ran through one suburb after another. They were going to look at some Siamese kittens which had been advertised in the Cape Argus. The house was not very easy to find. It was in fact a small holding of sorts, located near the cemetery, but nearer the flat marshy ground which abutted Zeekoei Vlei. The kittens, of which there were five, were twelve weeks old, and so cute and adorable that the brothers fell in love with all five of them. But they could take just one kitten home with them. After cuddling them all in turn, it was Alexander who said 'This one is smaller than the others. We should take him.'

'Yes, let's do that,' Roy agreed.

'Right,' their mother said. 'That's the one for us then.'

All the way back home, a journey of almost an hour in duration, the boys in the Vauxhall's back seat juggled the compliant kitten between the two of them. The little creature miaowed in a tiny, high pitched voice, but it purred also. Once again, it was Alexander who took the initiative, this time in naming the kitten. 'Let's call him Simba!' he said.

'That's a good name for a cat,' Mr. Maclean agreed. And Simba he became.

The brothers adored their kitten. They played with him, and cuddled him, and rolled ping pong balls for the little animal to chase, and twiddled feathers they found in their wanderings for the kitten to leap up at. Their mother fed the rapidly growing kitten finely chopped cuts of beef, and chopped up sheep kidneys and liver. She also gave it a bowl of milk every day. Within the first week of ownership of the little cat, she and the boys had taken it to the vet for its second inoculations and a general checkup. Simba grew up surrounded by loving attention and happiness, and he became a very handsome cat, his rich dark brown Siamese markings displayed to advantage by the creamy pale fur of the rest of his coat. His eyes were a lustrous, deep blue in colour. He developed the typically raucous Siamese voice, and he was clearly very fond of the brothers, playing happily with them, and following them into the garden, where he would frequently stay close by them.

Even Alexander's father, who wasn't really a cat man, preferring dogs, became fond of Simba. He admired his bold self assurance and his doggish manner. The first time Stewart visited, with his shaggy dog in tow, Simba emitted a baby hiss and fluffed himself up and stood his ground. The dog, somewhat alarmed by this strangely coloured creature with bright blue eyes and a threatening hiss, kept its distance. Stewart's dog became even more cautious as Simba grew up.

'That's some cat you've got there Sandy!' Stewart declared, one Saturday morning in early May.

Alexander laughed. 'Your dog thinks so!'

'We're going to get clay from the river to make bricks,' Alexander told Stewart. 'Are you coming?'

Alexander had conceived of multiple moulds made from plywood from which to cast tiny oblong toy bricks from a deposit of thick creamy clay on the banks of the stream. Roy had used his fretsaw to cut the plywood into the correct shapes, and the pieces slotted together, and could be taken apart easily, freeing the clay bricks, which were then lined up to bake in the sun. Stewart and the two brothers clambered over the fence at the bottom of the garden, and made their way through the undergrowth to the stream. All three boys soon had streaks of creamy clay and red mud smeared on their shoes, arms and legs. They had a bucket and a garden trowel with them, to scoop the soft clay out of the banks of the stream.

'What are you going to build with the bricks, Sandy?' Stewart asked.

'Forts. For our toy soldiers.'

Dirt-smeared and happy, the boys returned with the load of clay to the back garden, where they had a wonderful time breaking off and shaping lumps of clay with their fingers, then pressing them into the moulds. The Maclean brothers were wearing shoes, which were by then wet and filthy. Stewart, more sensibly for the task, was wearing sandals over bare feet.

They laid out the moulds in the sun. 'We'll come back once

the clay begins to dry, and get the bricks out of the moulds,' Alexander said.

Stewart had cut down one of the long slim saplings which abounded between the fence and the river. He had stripped the leaves from it, then, using his folding pocket knife, he had peeled away the thin bark, showing up the white, slightly oily wood beneath. He cut the final one and a half feet off the thin top end of the stem, and was left with a sturdy, somewhat flexible length of about three feet long which glistened palely in the sunlight.

'What are you going to do with that, Stewart?' asked Roy.

'I'll make a bow. I can use the smaller sticks to make arrows.'

'Oh – lend me your pocket knife, Stewart! I want to go cut a piece off too!' exclaimed Alexander.

'Me too!' said Roy.

'Well … OK.' Stewart handed Alexander the pocket knife, which had a genuine bone handle, and all three boys clambered back over the fence, and made their way into the thickets of long stemmed saplings. Stewart had already shown himself the expert in this endeavour, so the Maclean brothers allowed him to advise them as to what saplings to cut, and where. Within a very short while all three boys were mock sword-fighting with each other, shrieking and laughing.

'What's going on down there?' yelled Mr. Maclean from halfway up the garden. He walked to the bottom of the garden, as the boys climbed back over the fence.

The boys showed him their sticks, explaining what they intended. Alexander's father said 'Come with me, I'll show you how to bind them with string,' and the boys followed him to the veranda. 'Wait here. I'll fetch some string.'

The Maclean brothers' father showed the boys how to bind the sticks securely for a length of about nine inches in the centre. 'Now we can notch the ends of the sticks and string them.'

He took Alexander's stick, and borrowing Stewart's pocket knife, he cut a downward facing notch into one end of the stick, an inch down from the tip. Then he cut a long length of string, fastened it in the notch he had cut, wrapped it around the tip of the stick a few times and tied it in a knot. The string dangled loose.

'There,' he said. 'Now you chaps can do the rest. I'll leave you the ball of string.'

Chapter Three

Alexander was in the same class at school as Stewart. This meant that from the beginning, he had a friend in his class, and Stewart's popularity with the other boys meant that Alexander was included in their group. Alexander was only to begin to dislike school a year or two into high school. Alexander joined the school choir, which was conducted by a middle aged teacher named Miss Armstrong. Alexander was taught, for the first time, how to breathe when he sang; how to take air into the very depths of his lungs, down to his belly, using his diaphragm muscles, and how to expel the breath in a steady, even, controlled manner. He was taught how to open his throat and to project his voice. He was taught how to sustain a single high note for what he would once have thought was an impossible length of time. Alexander derived huge pleasure from singing. His treble was unusually pure and powerful. In school concerts he always had one or more solos to sing. He stood now with the choir in the front of the hall during morning assembly. Alexander's father had a fine tenor voice, and he too enjoyed singing. Alexander's mother, however, while appreciating music up to a point, was tone deaf, and she could not sing in key. Yet her natural speaking voice was pleasant, and it had none of the stridency that some women seem born to.

Alexander disliked soccer. He was to find as he grew older that he disliked all team sports. He never knew what to do with the ball on the rare occasions he found himself in possession of it. His only other dread at school was Maths. Again, he had no feeling for it. The logic of mathematics evaded him. He enjoyed History and English classes most of all, along with art classes and choir practice.

Alexander was taught cursive script for the first time in his life. He and his classmates were taught using old fashioned steel nib dipping pens of the type which had been used by Victorian solicitors' clerks, being provided with metal inkwells which fitted into a round hole at the top right hand corner of the individual wooden desks that each pupil sat at. Later that year the class was instructed to buy fountain pens. Pelikan was the favoured brand, as it was not too costly a fountain pen. Alexander enjoyed using his Pelikan fountain pen. To refill it with ink, you unscrewed the casing to the barrel, and revealed a stubby shaft which, when you dipped the pen into a bottle of ink, and revolved this shaft with your fingers, operated a plunger which rose slowly and drew the ink into the pen's ink chamber. Then you screwed the barrel's casing back on.

Alexander developed a flowing, rather florid cursive script, which he was to retain fundamentally unchanged for the rest of his life. Roy, in standard two, had not yet been taught cursive script, or as he called it "joined-up writing." He looked forward to being taught cursive script, as he too wished to own a fountain pen, which he anticipated his parents buying for him as soon as he reached standard three and began to learn cursive writing.

Some of the children, especially the boys, succeeded in making a horrible mess of themselves when they were taught cursive script using steel nib dipping pens. Stewart was rather messy in this regard. The joy of flicking inky balled up paper pellets at each other was quickly discovered, even though to be caught indulging in this practice meant having the open palm of your hand struck twice with a heavy wooden ruler. Alexander was neat. He barely got the tips of his first two fingers and thumb inked up when he used a dipping pen, or later, a fountain pen.

'How do you keep your fingers so clean, Sandy?' Stewart asked him.

'I don't know,' Alexander replied. 'I'm just careful, I suppose.'

Sometimes Stewart brought his homework round to the Maclean house, and he and Alexander tackled their homework together. Stewart did not find Maths difficult, and he tried to show his friend how to cope with Maths problems. Alexander in turn tried to communicate something of his enthusiasm for English and History, in seeking to explain what seemed incomprehensible to Stewart, in as simple terms as he could. But even if they were not able to entirely overcome each other's mental blocks, the boys enjoyed being together. But just as often as Alexander and Stewart formed a duo, Roy would also join them in their outdoors play. Yet Stewart remained far more Alexander's friend than he did Roy's.

In late May it grew much cooler, and the first rains of the coming winter arrived. Throughout the winter months of June, July and August, cold fronts would envelope the Peninsula in low cloud and continuous rain for days, sometimes even for a week or two at a time. Alexander's parents went to OK Bazaars on Main Road and bought four small electric two-bar incandescent heaters; one each was kept in each bedroom, and one in the sitting room. These constituted the only heating in the house unless Mr. Maclean lighted a fire in the sitting room fireplace. This he did not do nearly often enough for Alexander, who loved a fire burning in the grate. Alexander did not understand why his father was so set against an open fire. After all, Dorcas would clean up the cold grey ash the following morning. Perhaps Alexander's father did not like the fine deposit of grey soot on every surface in the sitting room that cleaning the fireplace caused. Maybe Alexander's father, born in hot, sultry, equatorial Mombasa, and growing up in a warm climate even during his school years in the equatorial Kenya Highlands, simply could not get to grips mentally with the idea of cold weather.

'Oh Dad, please can't we have a fire tonight?' Alexander would beg his father, but he rarely got his way. So the family huddled in front of one of the tiny electric heaters in the evenings, and Alexander hated the cold and damp, and he caught chest infections, and suffered distressing attacks of asthma. That first winter in Cape Town, Alexander seemed to have to spend a lot of time in bed. He was often absent from school. He suffered frequent attacks of asthma, which were treated with aminophylline tablets or syrup. The red-dyed aminophylline syrup had a vile taste, and Alexander referred to it, with a shudder, as "red *dhawa*." (*Dhawa* being Swahili for medicine).

The little boy learned long before his time what the fear of dying felt like. He learned that exerting control over his mental state and outlook when ill with asthma was very important, for by doing so he could minimize the impact of the attacks. He dared not allow the fear of asphyxiation to induce panic, as that would only worsen the attack. He was in these respects a very grown up little boy, at an age when most children have never had to trouble themselves with learning how to behave like grownups. Alexander grew immensely close to his mother, whom he associated with comfort and healing when he was suffering one of these all too frequent bouts of chest infection and asthma that winter. It was a closeness which would persist until the end of his mother's life, no matter how far he might be physically removed from his mother.

Alexander would already have matriculated and left school, before salbutamol inhalers became available in South Africa. Thereafter he never left home without his Ventolin inhaler in his pocket. Alexander suffered his last bad asthma attack in 1978, when he was aged twenty-three. Thereafter, although he would experience mild asthma-like symptoms throughout his life whenever he caught a chest infection, he would never again have cause to be as scared as he had so often had reason to be as a child.

Stewart visited Alexander two or three times during these periods in bed. Stewart and Alexander would look at each other, each as stuck for words as the other. Eventually Stewart said 'I wish you could see the river. It's twice as wide and twice as fast as usual.'

'We'll go look at it together as soon as I can get up again, Stewart.'

The two boys, Alexander sitting up in bed and leaning back against the pillows, Stewart sitting on the chair at Alexander's desk, continued in silence a while longer, a silence that was both companionable, yet somewhat awkward, then Stewart said 'Get well soon. I'll come see you again sometime.'

'Thanks. Bye.'

'Bye Sandy,' and Stewart would leave.

By early September, spring was on its way. Alexander and his brother climbed over their garden fence and followed the course of the river downstream, until they were behind the older houses further up Mallaig Road. Here there were big old trees overhanging the stream. Beneath them grew clumps of magnificent arum lilies, their pure white flowers unfurling like trumpet mouths from the thick stamens laden with bright yellow pollen. These lilies were the most impressive blooms Alexander had ever seen. Neither brother thought of picking them; it would have seemed a desecration. The two boys walked to the end of Mallaig Road sometimes, where the tar merged into a dirt track, and the *veld* across the river was a mass of lovely blue lupins in bloom. It was one of the most beautiful sights Alexander had ever seen, as if the blue sky had decided to spread itself across the ground. He and Roy used the stepping stones to cross the river and gathered an armful of blooms each and took them back to their mother, who stuck the long stems with their multitude of blossoms on each stem in vases with water. The house was full of blue lupins.

By mid September, with the sun shining from a sky whose colour reminded Alexander of the family's kitchen crockery from Kenya, it was warm enough for Alexander and his brother to play outside in their shirt sleeves. One Sunday after lunch, the Maclean family, along with Stewart Fleming, got into the car and drove to Kirstenbosch Gardens, the world famous mountainside botanical gardens above Bishopscourt. Alexander was enraptured by the beauty of these gardens, with the dramatic mountain crags looming over them. He had as yet no conscious awareness of how susceptible he was to natural beauty, but this love of Nature and of the wild places in the world would become stronger and more consciously informed as he grew older, and it was to remain with him all his life.

Pathways wound between magnificent shrubberies, floral displays and trees. Alexander, Roy and Stewart ran ahead of the adults up the winding pathways, eager to see the next wonderful sights unfold. The astonishing avenue of camphor trees, with their multitude of twisted, writhing, smooth barked branches growing from low down near the ground, and meeting high above the avenue, amazed all three boys.

The top left quarter of the Gardens was given over to *fynbos* and proteas, acting as a lure for the sunbirds. Sipping with their long narrow curved bills from the spectacular King Protea blossoms (South Africa's national flower) and from the ericas, with their profuse blossoms in shades of pink, cream and white, were dozens of tiny, hugely colourful sunbirds, of which those with iridescent green backs, creamy bellies, and double half-collars of the brightest scarlet and the deepest blue across the top of their breasts, seemed to Alexander to be the loveliest. The little creatures, like costume jewellery taken flight, their colours flashing in the sunlight, would hover motionless above a blossom, their wings a blur, or hang upside down from a stem as they probed the multi-floreate ericas with their long bills. Once Alexander had left school, and the family (then living in Johannesburg) had returned to live in Cape Town again, he was to spend entire days hiking alone in the mountains, and by then he could recognise and name the individual species of sunbirds. The Southern Double-Collared Sunbird, with its scarlet and blue banded half collars, and the Orange-Breasted Sunbird, with a half collar of Tyrean purple, were the two species of sunbirds which had first made such an impression on Alexander during this, his earliest visit to Kirstenbosch, and they remained his favourites.

'Oh Mum! This is the most beautiful place I've ever seen!' exclaimed Alexander, a grin of sheer delight on his face.

Olivia Maclean smiled at her eldest son, and for a moment, she was afraid for him. She hoped he was not going to be too badly hurt when he grew up, by all the man-made ugliness there was in the world.

The Maclean family, along with Stewart, sat at a table on the cafeteria terrace at half past four. The adults ordered coffees, and the boys, as a treat, were allowed ice cream cones with a stick of flaky chocolate stuck in the ice cream. Cape White-eyes, Cape Bulbuls and sunbirds flitted and hovered amidst the proteas and the shrubbery alongside the terrace.

In Nairobi, the Macleans had employed a live-in cook, a live in houseboy, a live-in kitchen *toto*, and a gardener who worked five days a week. Their house had been larger than the house in Mallaig Road, and the garden had covered an acre of ground, rather than the current quarter acre, but the Macleans had not truly needed three full time domestic servants. But in Kenya, everyone had servants, and lots of them, and it had not occurred to the boys' parents, themselves brought up in households with many servants, to behave any differently.

Accustomed to servants, the boy's mother had hired Dorcas, who worked Monday to Friday from twenty to eight in the morning (she came in early so that the boys could get off to school) until five in the afternoon, and she worked Saturday mornings also. Mrs. Maclean had not paused to question whether she needed a full time domestic servant. Had Mrs. Maclean asked herself that question, the correct answer might have been 'No, I do not need a servant working as many hours as Dorcas does: there is not enough work for her.'

However, it was pleasant for Mrs. Maclean not to have to slave over domestic tasks, although she still had to prepare supper every evening (but Dorcas' first task of the day was to do the washing up from the supper the night before, and often, Dorcas would have made the supper which only needed heating up by Mrs. Maclean). Dorcas cleaned and dusted and hoovered the house every day. She made the beds, and she did the laundry and the ironing. She washed up the dirty dishes. She served Mrs. Maclean cups of tea and coffee during the day, and she baked cakes and biscuits – a function the brothers much appreciated, as did their mother, to whom baking did not come naturally.

Olivia Maclean enjoyed gardening, and with little housework to attend to, she was able to spend much more time in the garden, which she was rapidly turning into a true garden, rather than merely a lawn. The American plane tree had taken well. By the coming of spring, flowerbeds (dug out by Joseph the gardener on Friday mornings) lined the perimeter of almost the entire garden, as well as the exterior of the low garden wall. Within the first month of the family moving to Mallaig Road, Olivia Maclean had planted hydrangeas on the shady side of the house, and roses, geraniums and cannas elsewhere. She also planted a dark pink bougainvillea which she intended training up the corner pillar supporting the roof above the veranda. With the arrival of spring in September, Mrs. Maclean planted dahlias, gladiolus and begonias. Bordering the flowerbeds, she planted marigolds, petunias, nasturtiums, hyacinths, freesias, pansies, irises, and other British garden flowers.

During the three winter months, when rain often kept the boys indoors, Roy built machines and bridges with his Meccano set, these projects laid out on the parquet floor of his bedroom. Alexander too enjoyed using Meccano, but he lacked the dedication and inventiveness with these pieces of pressed and perforated metal (which came in red, green, or occasionally, yellow or blue), and with the tiny nuts and bolts used to fasten them, that Roy possessed. Instead, Alexander built houses and forts using both Minibricks (a toy building system of rubber bricks), and the clay bricks the boys had baked under the sun. Alexander also spent hours at his small desk drawing architectural plans, and cross-sections of motor cars and steam locomotives. These latter were highly inventive and creative: although Alexander's comprehension of the internal combustion engine, and of steam power, was crude in the extreme, he applied what he knew to extremely imaginative vehicles which shared some qualities with the creations of W. Heath Robinson. Creating these designs brought Alexander even more pleasure than reading: through his drawings and designs, he could escape the restrictions and limitations of real life, exchanging them for the limitless opportunities afforded by his imagination.

Alexander had always drawn, and painted in watercolours also. As early as six years old, at a watering stop on the Nairobi – Mombasa railway line, he had sketched the enormous Garratt steam locomotive that was hauling the train the family was travelling on, on their way to holiday on the coast. His mother kept these early drawings, and in his late middle age, Alexander was to find them among his mother's possessions.

For Alexander, reading was also an escape, especially when he was lying sick in bed, leaning back against the pillows. When he was well he lay on his stomach on his bed and read; he read much more than most boys his age. He was too young yet to read the stirring adventure novels by G. A. Henty, which dated from the late nineteenth century, or the novels being written by that newly prominent Scottish writer of historical fiction, Nigel Tranter. He was to come to these writers in his early teens, but he deeply enjoyed children's non-fiction books about ships and the sea, and one of his favourite books was a lavishly illustrated history of sailors and mariners, and their ships. He read and re-read many times *The Wonder Book of How it's Done*, *The Wonder Book of Motors*, and *The Wonder Book of Daring Deeds*, all of which had belonged to his father as a boy, the first two titles' inside covers covered in cartoon figures engaged in hilarious and often disastrous activities. By the time he was eleven years old, Alexander had read Rudyard Kipling's *Kim* for himself, and he was to reread the story a number of times, well into his adulthood, each time gaining something new from it. One of his earliest memories was of being read to by his mother from Kipling's *Just So Stories*, each story of which described how a particular animal acquired its distinctive features. *The Elephant's Child* was his favourite story, for Alexander could relate strongly to it. Like the Elephant's Child in the story, he too had a number of strong minded and domineering aunts. *The Just So Stories* were wry and charming, and they made Alexander and his mother laugh. Alexander continued to enjoy them into his adulthood.

Nor had Alexander quite outgrown the sweet stories of very early childhood, such as Beatrix Potter's stories about *Peter Rabbit* and other animals of the English countryside, and A. A. Milne's stories about *Winnie the Pooh*. Arthur Mee's arrangement for children of stories from the Bible was an old favourite of his, as were Charles and Mary Lamb's stories from Shakespeare, with their beautiful illustrations by that incomparable illustrator of an earlier age, Arthur Rackham. Alexander read and reread *The*

Princess and the Goblin, by George MacDonald, and its sequel, *The Princess and Curdie*, both published in the 1870s, which were illustrated with black and white sketches by Arthur Hughes. On one level, these were simply wonderful adventure stories, but on another, they were rich in symbolism, and although so young, Alexander was already dimly aware of this. He was to love these stories all his life. Alexander's mother introduced him to the *Just William* series of children's stories, written by Richmal Crompton between the wars, about William, a middle class English schoolboy who lives in the English countryside, and with whose adventures, and struggles against adult tyranny, Alexander could identify.

Alexander's mother had also read to him from *The Wind in the Willows*, by Kenneth Grahame, set in pastoral Edwardian England, which Alexander was to read for himself for the first time at the house in Mallaig Road. He enjoyed it for its gentle mockery of Toad's failings and pretensions, and for the deeper meaning he had begun to discern in the tale of adventure, friendship and morality. Chapter seven, *"The Piper at the Gates of Dawn"*, moved Alexander tremendously when his mother first read it to him, although he did not then begin to understand why this was so, but as he grew older he was to identify on a far deeper level with the pantheism represented in the story by the god Pan, that keeper of all the wild places and their creatures. In his manhood, Alexander was to come to love and cherish the wilderness; those places where Man was incidental, rather than central, to Creation.

Alexander's childhood reading had almost nothing whatsoever to do with Africa. Although he lived in Africa, the world he escaped to when he read fiction was set largely in England; a pre-war England, or even an Edwardian England. It was this early exposure via fiction to an idealised, generally pastoral England, which explained Alexander's eagerness once he had left school to travel to England. While the Maclean family had been living in Kenya, they had twice travelled to England by sea on holiday (Alexander could remember the second voyage), but Alexander had to wait until he was twenty years old before he first visited England without his parents and brother.

Chapter Four

Alexander's paternal grandparents lived in the seaside village of
Kommetjie in an old, high ceilinged, single story house built of
stone, and roofed in corrugated iron painted green. Kommetjie
was a tiny village on the far side of the Peninsula from Fish Hoek,
on the shores of the cold Atlantic. There was no natural harbour;
the village (unlike Hout Bay further up the coast) was not a
fishing village, although a few fishermen engaged in line fishing
for white steenbras, stumpnose, tuna and albacore from small
boats that were hauled onto the beach when not in use. No, for
the most part the village housed retirees and artists and summer
holiday home visitors, along with some residents such as Rory
Maclean who, although working in Cape Town, wished to live
far from the city.

In the summertime, surfers descended on Long Beach, and
there was a steady traffic through the village of young people with
toned, tanned bodies and bleached, curly hair, who would arrive
in their old cars and Volkswagen Kombis and *bakkies* and vans.
Some of these youngsters would camp overnight amidst the groves
of white milkwood trees; others would camp in the dunes. The
Kommetjie Hotel off-licence did a good trade in the summer.

A wide, roofed stoep, covered in purple bougainvillea, embraced two sides of Alexander's grandparents' house, and there was a well established garden surrounded by a plastered, four foot high, white painted wall, in which hydrangeas in particular flourished, for they liked the sandy soil. Inside, the house was furnished for the most part with sturdy hardwood furniture, handmade in Kenya colony by Muslim Indian *fundis*, pieces which gleamed with polish and the patina of age, but there were some rather fine antique items of furniture also, which, like the dark, ancient oil paintings on the walls had come to Alexander's grandmother, Jeanie, from her father, a *tighearna* or laird from the Isle of Mull, who had emigrated with his family to Kenya a few years after Rory Maclean, his mother, sister and two younger brothers had joined their father in Kenya. Rory Maclean's father, also named Alexander, had been raised on a small farm, and his family had been tenants of Jeanie's family. Rory's father had been to agricultural college at Edinburgh, and he had become a tea planter in India. Soon after the First World War he had moved from India to Kenya to experiment with growing tea in the new colony. Jeanie's father had farmed many acres in the Kenya Highlands.

Jeanie Maclean, in her late fifties, sometimes spoke the Gaelic to her husband, for both had grown up familiar with the language which, during their childhood (and for a generation afterwards), was commonly spoken by the people of the Western Isles. She was a woman of pronounced opinions, much given in later life, through letters to the newspapers and via membership of earnest societies with high ideals, to conducting crusades against what she perceived to be moral and other dangers to South African society. She was at the forefront, for example, of the anti-fluoridation campaign in South Africa, and she frequently wrote letters about what she saw as a pervasive sexual immorality in South Africa. Her family had belonged to the Scottish Episcopal Church, and Jeanie Maclean possessed somewhat evangelical Christian moral principles. She deplored the influence of what she saw as a European and American permissive society on South African life. She and her husband attended services at the Presbyterian church in Fish Hoek. Rory had been raised a Catholic, but possessing as a young man no strong sense of religious feeling, he had left the Catholic Church on marrying Jeanie. It was some years later, while Alexander's father had been a boy in Mombasa, that Alexander's grandparents had ceased attending services at Mombasa's Church of England Cathedral, and had begun to attend Church of Scotland services instead. Rory and his wife had become firm Presbyterians, and he was later to become an elder in the Fish Hoek Presbyterian congregation.

Jeanie loved all her grandchildren fiercely, and that love was reciprocated. Alexander, named after his father (who was in turn named after his own grandfather), was her eldest grandchild. Both the Maclean boys looked forward tremendously to visiting their grandparents, which they and their family usually did on a Sunday afternoon. Alexander found the drive there exciting. It was a long drive, following Main Road through a largely urban landscape. Newlands, Claremont and Kenilworth were comfortable suburbs with old established homes, but the surroundings became less and less alluring as Alexander's family drove past Wynberg, Plumstead, Diep River and Retreat, before reaching False Bay at last at Muizenberg. From Muizenberg onwards the drive became filled with interest for Alexander, as it hugged the shores of False Bay (following what was generally thought of as the Indian Ocean shore of the Cape Peninsula), and Alexander enjoyed the proximity of the sea, which, in the wintertime, could be wild and storm tossed. But the summer sun of November shone down on the sea now, and the scattered white horses whipped up by the wind signalled a strong south-easter blowing. As they drove through Saint James, Alexander would peer at the grand old mansions on the hillside above the bay, in one of which, so his grandmother had told him – a huge white mansion with many Cape Dutch gables, and a profuse number of tall chimneys – she had stayed as a girl on holiday with her family, down from Kenya, for her father had been a friend of the owner.

Saint James was followed by Kalk Bay, with its working fishing harbour, and from the main road as you drove by, you could see the boats in the harbour, a scene Alexander, with his love of boats, always anticipated with pleasure. In the summertime a section of the beach at Kalk Bay would be crowded with Cape Coloured bathers, for the beach had a Coloured bathing area. Alexander was already acutely aware, notwithstanding his familiarity with Dorcas, the family servant, of the vast social and cultural gulf between Cape Coloured people and Europeans, and the sight of those brown bodies in the sun, so crowded together on the small section of beach given over to them, but otherwise behaving just like white folk at the beach, worked a strange fascination on him.

At Fish Hoek, a staid, middle class seaside town with a fine beach of white sand, and a number of small hotels and boarding houses and a variety of shops, along with a primary school, a high school, and churches of various denominations, Alexander's father took the Kommetjie road out of town, rather than keeping straight on for Simons Town, and the family cut across the Peninsula, which at this point was only a few miles wide. The Kommetjie road was a long, almost straight, narrow road with wide gravel verges, lined with flowering eucalyptus trees. Long dirt tracks and driveways opened periodically off the main road, giving access to small farms and small holdings. Kommetjie was located on the far side of the Peninsula, on the shores of the Atlantic Ocean.

'*Mo ghràidhean*! How are my boys?' Jeanie Maclean greeted her two grandsons. She gave each a kiss and a hug. Alexander, as he always did on entering his grandparents' home, went and sat cross legged on the leopard skin rug in front of the fireplace, staring fascinated at the snarling head with its huge fangs, and running his fingers against the direction of the hair on the pelt, thinking how tough and coarse the coat was compared to that of Simba. Granny Jeanie brought him and his brother a large cardboard box in which were some Schuco clockwork toy cars and a selection of other toy cars, all of which had belonged to their father as a boy. Alexander's father joined his sons for a few minutes, smiling as he looked at these old favourites from his childhood.

Rory Maclean was a big man, two or three years older than Jeanie, clean shaven, with swept back greying hair. He was an engineer by profession, and he worked for the Cape Town Municipality. He commuted between Kommetjie and the city five days a week, his wife driving him to Fish Hoek Station in the old Morris Oxford, where he caught the train into Cape Town. He still spoke with a trace of his soft Western Isles accent, an accent far removed from the music hall Scottish of popular imagination.

'Hullo Grandpa,' Alexander greeted him.

'Hullo Sandy. How are you?' his grandfather responded.

'Fine thanks. How are you, Grandpa?'

'I do well enough, lad.'

'Would you boys like some shortbread?' their grandmother asked them.

'Ooh – yes please!'

Both the brothers were very fond indeed of Granny Jeanie's rich shortbread. They began gorging themselves until their mother put a stop to their indulgences.

'Sandy – Roy! That's enough now! You've had enough of Granny's shortbread. You'll make yourselves sick at this rate. Go play outside for a while.'

The brothers went outside and began to chase each other around the garden, before breaking off their game to look inside their grandfather's workshop, which Roy in particular found fascinating. While they were doing so, their aunts on their father's side arrived. (Mary Scott and Margaret Boyd, along with their children – James and Tom, Mary's sons, who were aged nine and seven, and Jenny, aged five, and Mary, just three years old, who were Margaret's daughters – together with Margaret's husband, William). Both families lived in Upper Constantia on the slopes of the mountain, in a sprawling nineteenth century mansion, Hohenstein, which Mary Scott had bought in 1963 after her husband, a wealthy Kenya farmer and white hunter, had died on a hunting safari, and which she, her sister and her sister's husband ran as a shabby but delightful one star hotel catering mostly for long term residential guests. Alexander, Roy, James and Tom ran down the street towards the sea, not before Alexander had shouted at the adults, who were now sitting on the *stoep* 'We're going to look at the rock pool!'

The tide was fairly high. Sometimes interesting fish would be stranded in the rock pool, which some people swam in, but which looked dark and uninviting to Alexander, especially as he and his brother and a bunch of other boys had once gawked with fascinated horror at a five foot long shark that had been stranded in the rock pool after high tide, and was swimming around looking (to Alexander) like the embodiment of oceanic danger. At low tide in the warm weather the entire shoreline at Kommetjie stank powerfully of kelp rotting in the sun; you could sometimes smell Kommetjie long before you could see the village. On the way back, James, who always had more money than Alexander or Roy, bought five cents worth of Chappies bubblegum, and he gave each of the Maclean brothers a square of the hard pink gum. The boys arrived back at their grandparents' home blowing sickly pink bubbles.

'Sandy! Roy! You know you're not supposed to use bubblegum,' their mother exclaimed. 'How much have you got? Give it to me, please.'

'Oh Mum, James just gave us one piece each!'

'Well, spit it out and throw it in the dustbin.'

'Aww Mum …' But both Maclean boys removed their bubblegum and disposed of it in the bin in the kitchen.

Mary Scott smiled at her sons. 'Perhaps that's enough bubblegum for now. It is n't nice in front of other people, boys.'

The four boys ran back into the garden and commenced a game of tag. The adults chatted and drank their tea, or coffee, although Alexander's father and his Uncle William both had a lager. All four women ate some of the shortbread the Maclean brothers had earlier been gorging themselves on. The sun shone. The wind did not blow as strongly on this side of the peninsula. It was very warm.

In the late afternoon the Macleans drove back home the long way round, because the entire Maclean family enjoyed the drive, as a refreshing change from the urbanized Main Road, and the boys found it extremely exciting. Some distance along the Kommetjie road as it headed back towards Fish Hoek, they turned off the road to the left and drove through Noordhoek, where Alexander's Aunt Margaret stabled her two horses, and the road climbed to the start of the world renowned Chapman's Peak Drive, a narrow, winding, scenic route which hugged the cliffside high above the Atlantic, and connected Noordhoek with the fishing town of Hout Bay, about seven miles away. Alexander was always thrilled by this drive, just a low stone wall between the car and the cruel, rock-fanged sea far below. He caught a sight of the weathered, dark green, bronze leopard sitting atop Leopard's Rock, gazing out at the limitless ocean, just before the descent to Hout Bay began, and he felt happy. From Hout Bay you could drive into Cape Town, past Llandudno, Bakoven, Camps Bay, Clifton and Sea Point. Llandudno, Camps Bay and Clifton had very fine beaches whose sand was the palest gold in colour. Alternatively, you could take the Constantia Nek route from Hout Bay, and once through the *nek*, or pass, which cut through the mountain spine which ran for much of the length of the Peninsula, you descended to the suburbs on the far side of the mountain and then home to Rondebosch. The Macleans followed the winding ascent for Constantia Nek, which was the same route Alexander's aunts and their families would take on their way back to the hotel above Constantia.

Alexander was only ten years old, and he could barely have articulated his feelings for the Cape Peninsula – for its glorious vistas of mountain and sea, and its dramatic, exciting drives – but he was very much aware of the beauty of the region, and he loved it, and he would come to miss the Cape Peninsula terribly when, in early 1968, the Maclean family had to move to Johannesburg. Alexander would return with his family to live in Cape Town after matriculating from high school, and for the rest of his life, no matter where he was in the world, he would measure a region's natural and scenic beauty by what he remembered of the Cape Peninsula.

As the brothers and their parents entered their home, Simba greeted them with a raucous, wailing miaow, and Alexander scooped him up and hugged him. 'Did you miss us, you poor pussy?' he asked the cat. The chocolate and cream coloured cat purred throatily and rubbed its face against Alexander's cheek. Mrs. Maclean went to the kitchen, to prepare the little animal's supper. Her husband looked into the kitchen. 'I'll pour you a sherry, shall I, Livia?' he asked.

'Yes please Darling,' his wife replied.

Mr. Maclean went to the drinks cabinet in the sitting room and poured his wife a sherry and himself a single scotch. After putting Simba's supper on the kitchen floor at his feeding corner, Olivia Maclean went through to the sitting room and joined her husband, who handed her a small glass of sherry. 'Cheers,' he said, and sat down with his whiskey.

A little distance up Golden Grove Road, in a single story house with a rather overgrown garden, lived Mrs. Irwin. She was as ugly as a witch in a children's fairy story, old and bent and alone, her husband long dead, her children flown. Sometimes, on their way home from school in the afternoon, Alexander and his brother would see her in her front garden, standing and watching the children as they walked and ran and cycled by.

'There's that old witch,' Alexander said to Roy, walking home from school the next day.

'She does look like a witch,' Roy replied.

'Uurrghr … I wonder if she could put a spell on you?' Alexander asked.

The brothers hurried by, leaving Mrs. Irwin staring after them.

The Maclean clan decided to have a family Christmas at the Hohenstein Hotel. Mary Scott enjoyed preparing big meals. She was an inspired and enthusiastic cook, and the dishes she served were often memorable. More than anything else, it was Mary Scott's cooking which retained the loyalty of her guests, some of whom had been with her since she had first opened the old mansion as a hotel.

Round about the fifteenth of December, Mrs. Maclean and her sons began to make paper chains from brightly coloured paper, sitting at the dining room table, which had been covered with an old bed sheet, with sheets of coloured paper, a pot of glue and several pairs of scissors to hand. Alexander and Roy entered into the secular spirit of Advent with enthusiasm, and the brothers and their mother turned out great long chains of bright green and yellow and red and orange paper decorations. These were then hung in the sitting room and the dining room, fastened in shallow swags just beneath the ceiling from the corners of the room to the light fixture in the centre of the ceiling, and so to the opposite corners. From the light fitting in the middle of the ceiling in the sitting room, their mother suspended a glorious old bell-shaped decoration, very large and brightly coloured, which complemented the handmade paper chains.

On Saturday the eighteenth of December, that year of 1965, the boys and their father drove to the garden centre in Kenilworth, where the brothers' excitement could hardly be contained, for they were going to buy the Christmas tree. Despite considering many different trees, it was Alexander's choice – as was so often the case – which carried the day. Alexander invariably cast the deciding vote when some small decision arose in the family. Why was this? Perhaps it was the strength of his will, which overrode all opposition. Perhaps it was simply that he was decisive, when others were still trying to make up their minds.

The tree was a living tree, its roots contained in a small wooden tub. It stood about four feet tall; five feet tall with the tub. After twelfth night had passed, Joseph would plant it out at the bottom of the garden. At the garden centre, Mr. Maclean arranged an old blanket on top of the Vauxhall's roof, and opening the windows an inch or so all around, he fed a length of clothes line through the windows and tied the tree down on the roof. In the late afternoon the family decorated the tree, the boys having tied little puffs of cotton wool along lengths of string, to simulate snow when festooned around the tree. The ancient and precious Christmas tree ornaments that had (Alexander assumed) always been in the family, for he could not remember a time at Christmas before them, were unpacked. They were of a quality and splendour harkening back to a previous age, for nothing of their quality was available in the shops anymore. They included a range of fragile, beautifully made ornaments which were packed in nests of cotton wool: globes, crescent moons, stars, bells, and small animals, in every colour imaginable, metallic colours which gleamed and shone in the light, and there were also a few tiny artificial birds made with real feathers, and a long string of miniature Christmas tree lights, and small coloured wax candles in holders, and a golden angel for the top of the tree.

These preparations for Christmas filled the brothers with excitement. There were delighted exclamations and happy laughter as the boys helped their mother unpack the decorations, a procedure which had acquired an almost ritual significance. Alexander could remember clearly as many as five Christmases back, all of those in Nairobi, and the happy assembly of bright paper chains, and the hanging of the ornaments on the Christmas tree, brought him a sense of comforting continuity. The ornaments were hung from the tips of the branches; the string of coloured lights was arranged in a spiral up the outside of the tree; small coloured wax candles in holders with spring loaded clips were fastened to the branches, and Roy, standing on a stepladder, attached the golden angel to the topmost point of the tree. The family stood back to admire the tree, and after supper, the boys could hardly contain themselves, waiting for it to grow dark, so that the little electric lights could be turned on.

'Ooh … it's lovely!' Alexander exclaimed, as the coloured lights blinked on and off, and the golden flames from the tiny candles burned clear and steady. His father ruffled Alexander's hair.

'It is pretty. What do you think, Livia?' Mr. Maclean asked his wife. 'Our first Christmas in South Africa.'

The boys' mother gave one of her rare smiles. 'I'm glad some things have n't changed,' she said.

Chapter Five

The Hohenstein mansion had been built in the 1890s by an immigrant German industrialist. He had not sought to recreate a German *schloss*, but had allowed the architect to draw his major creative inspiration from the Cape and British colonial architectural motifs which abounded in the region – indeed, they could be found in buildings right across the British Empire. Hohenstein, which had been built on the eastern slopes of the Table Mountain range, was a huge, rambling place of three stories, not counting the cellars and the topmost attics. The outer walls were plastered, painted white, although the paint was now peeling in places, and up beneath the eves, where the damp had got in, there were chunks of plaster missing. The house had tall chimneys and many gables; the gables on the main entrance façade were Cape vernacular in style, while those on the garden front were stepped. There was a covered veranda on the garden front, reaching the full length of the main house, with an open balcony above it and a wide terrace below it. The house looked out across lawns (often somewhat overgrown) and a vineyard, bordered by mature oak trees. The vineyard was let out, but it produced a wine marketed under the Hohenstein label. There was a magnificent view, looking across

Constantia. To the east lay the Cape Flats, and beyond them the soaring mountain ranges which guarded the Interior, and which were for so long a barrier to further exploration. To the south-east, False Bay's sparkling blue waters could be made out, with their backdrop of the far distant Hottentots Holland range, which in the winter would sometimes be capped with snow. Behind the house the mountain slope rose rather steeply, and the road wound its way up to Rhodes Drive, which it joined below one of the gates to the Cecilia forest plantation.

Mary Scott had come into a substantial inheritance on her husband's untimely death in the central African bush, and she had used some of it to buy Hohenstein, which was in poor repair, not having been inhabited for at least a decade. Alexander's aunt had had the most urgent structural work attended to, but even now, the big house had a neglected air, and there were several bedrooms on the second floor which had been effectively abandoned, their ceilings threatening to collapse, the damp having got in. These rooms were kept closed up, and the items of furniture in them – vast armoires, huge double beds, great overstuffed chairs and sofas, and inlaid dressing tables – were left uncovered even by dust sheets. Neither Mary Scott nor even the children knew exactly what might be found in the topmost attics: the children were nervous of exploring up there (although not as scared as they were of venturing into the cellars). The half dozen Coloured servants Mrs. Scott employed did not, as servants might have done in a previous age, live in the topmost attics. In the cellars there were some locked doors made of great sturdy planks of stinkwood, dark with age and grime, to which no one had found the keys, and what lay behind them remained unknown.

Alexander and his cousin James, a year younger than himself, had once ventured down into the cellars with torches, but beyond the main chamber (whose vaulted roof was merely a suggestion in the darkening gloom, and which housed an ancient and long disused furnace and boiler, with lumps of coal still littering the stone flagged floor), the sinister shadows either side of the narrow beams of the torches were so alarming, the smell of mildew and rot and decomposing matter so unpleasant, that both boys had quickly lost their nerve, and when James turned and fled for the stone steps leading up into the house, Alexander was fast on his heels.

On Christmas Day Alexander's family (his mother wearing a pretty floral print cotton dress with a full skirt, a tight waist and a close fitting bodice, with a small gold locket at her neck, and his father wearing grey flannels with sharp creases, a Maclean tartan tie, and a light sports jacket) joined Jeanie and Rory Maclean at Hohenstein during the morning. Alexander's Aunt Mary had a gift for each of her nephews, in Alexander's case, a large, beautifully illustrated children's book on the history of the motor car. The Maclean clan shared their Christmas Day with the five permanent residents at the hotel: an austere old gentleman who had a very inexpensive room high on the second floor, and four old ladies, two of whom shared a big first floor bedroom and two who had large first floor bedrooms to themselves. If any of these residents still possessed any living relatives, they were too distant either in fact or in sentiment to spend Christmas Day with them. There was also a family from England, the Oakleys, newly arrived immigrants to South Africa, whose two children, a boy and a girl, played with Alexander and his brother and his Scott cousins. Like the Maclean and the Scott boys, the English boy was wearing short trousers. The children ran shrieking up and down the rows of vines in the vineyard below the lawns, while the adults, minus Mary Scott, who was supervising the preparation of the Christmas lunch in the huge, high ceilinged old kitchen, sat on the covered veranda (too grand to be called a *stoep*) that ran the full length of the garden front of the house.

After a while the children came inside and began to race each other up and down the grand staircase, which was eight feet wide and built of European oak that had darkened with age, and whose banister had acquired a rich patina from more than seventy years of being grasped by many hands. The walls alongside the staircase were panelled in a paler wood, and via five separate turns, the staircase, only six feet wide between the first and the second floors, reached up as far as the third story. Then Alexander and Roy hung over the banister of the minstrels' gallery which overlooked the great hall, a space which rose through two stories and had dark wooden panelling reaching up to a height of about ten feet. Above the wooden panelling the walls were plastered and painted white, and hung with ancient oil paintings – portraits and landscapes – which had been there when Mary Scott had bought the house, and which were so darkened with age, and smoke from the fireplace, as to be reduced to the merest hints of human features, the suggestion only of distant country vistas. There was a huge baronial fireplace, inside which Alexander could stand upright in the summer and peer above him into the flue. This vast double story room displayed its most fulsome and welcoming character during the three or four cold, wet Cape winter months. Then a fire would be crackling and spitting in the wide grate, the aromatic scent of burning pine clean and cheering, and the walls would gleam softly at each lighted wall sconce set just below the top of the panelling, and on Saturday evenings in the wintertime there would be solo *artistes* or ensembles of country and folk singers booked by Mary Scott, which evenings then accounted for about three quarters of the bar-take during the winter. But Christmas falls in the southern hemisphere's midsummer, and although the interior of the old house, with its thick walls and high ceilings, was pleasantly cool, outside it was very warm indeed.

Miss Spence-Traggart, one of the old ladies, said to Alexander, who had entered the residents' drawing room, whose walls were papered in salmon pink and lime green, and whose fireplace was of white marble, 'My gosh, how you are growing. And what a good looking little boy you have become.'

Miss Grohen (whose name delighted Alexander, and could reduce him to fits of giggles, for it was pronounced "groan") said 'Happy Christmas dear. Which one are you?' By which Alexander correctly understood her to mean 'Whose child are you?'

Alexander replied 'Happy Christmas Miss Groan, my name is Alexander Maclean.'

Miss Grohen responded 'But you are all named Maclean, not so?'

'Oh no, Miss Groan. My cousins are Scotts and Boyds.' Then Alexander ran from the big room before the giggles overtook him; oh, how wonderful her name was!

Roy was now playing on the veranda with the battery powered New York Police Department motor tricycle, which had a wailing siren and a flashing light, which his grandparents had given him for Christmas. His cousin James was trying to persuade him to let him have a go. Alexander had brought with him his Christmas present from his parents earlier that morning. It was a very large model cargo ship, with four tiny wheels inset beneath the flat bottomed hull, but the ship could float. It had cargo hatchways which opened above each of the four holds, and working, swivelling derricks with which you could load cargo through the hatchways. He went to it, and saw that one of the derricks had been broken.

'Who broke this?' he cried. 'Who broke my ship?'

He saw Roy looking away, guilt written on his face. 'Did you break my ship?' Alexander accused his brother.

'I was trying to see if the crane would lift my police trike up. It broke.'

'You beast!' Alexander yelled. 'My beautiful ship!'

'I did n't mean to break it,' Roy responded.

'Why do you always break my things?' Alexander shouted. There were tears trembling on his lower lashes.

'I'm sorry.'

The adults, with the exception of Alexander's father, ignored this outburst. Alexander's father came and knelt down, and examined the broken derrick. 'I can fix this,' he told his sons. 'We'll fix it when we get home. Dont shout at Roy, Sandy. He did n't do it on purpose.'

Alexander's lower lip quivered for a minute, and he gave his brother a dirty look. But after a while he saw how downcast Roy was, so he went up to him and said 'It's alright Roy. I know you did n't mean it. Dad 'll fix it.'

Roy smiled at his older brother. 'Yeah. Dad can fix anything.'

The brothers were friends again, and the spirit of Christmas descended once more upon the gathering.

There were several dogs also on the veranda, ranging from a tiny Chihuahua, through a pug with bulbous, protuberant eyes, and an elderly spaniel with a rather high aroma, to a German shepherd with a slightly insane look on its face. On top of a table sat a very large tabby cat, and further down the veranda, Jenny, Margaret's eldest daughter, who was five years old, was cuddling a tortoiseshell cat whose five kittens were playing with a small ball.

A large brass gong which stood in an ebony wood frame on a table in the hallway was struck four times. The percussive reports echoed and boomed throughout the house, and could be heard on the veranda. The Coloured servant who had struck the gong appeared. She was wearing a white cap and a white apron over a black cotton dress which reached to her knees.

'*Merrem* says lunch is ready in the dining room.'

At first no one paid her any attention, so she raised her voice and repeated herself. Aunty Margaret then stood up and the others followed her, the children in a sudden rush ahead of the adults. Margaret Boyd raised her voice and said 'James! Tom! Slow down!'

Alexander's mother said 'You too, Sandy – Roy. Dont rush.'

The various members of the extended Maclean clan entered the great hall, followed by the Oakleys. The four old lady residents in their best outfits (Miss Grohen and one other old lady were wearing hats and gloves), and the old gentleman (wearing a Bishops' green and navy Old Diocesan Union tie and a dark blue blazer), appeared from the residents' drawing room, and (counting the children) eighteen people (with Mary Scott joining them from the kitchen) made their way into the enormous, high ceilinged dining room, whose fireplace was almost as big as that in the great hall. The Chihuahua, the pug and the spaniel followed the chattering group into the dining room and arranged themselves beneath and near the dining table. The room was dominated by the huge mahogany dining table, at least fifteen feet long and five feet wide, which was covered with starched white table cloths, and on top of which a large floral centrepiece was arranged in a big copper basin. Against the wall, between the two doors which gave access to the great hall, stood a massive, highly polished, carved sideboard and dresser of European oak darkened with age, with tall silver candlesticks at either end, and an impressive display of Spode dinnerware arranged above the wide serving top.

At each place setting was a paper party hat, which almost everyone, even the rather severe old gentleman resident, donned. The two old lady residents wearing hats of their own refused however to remove them. There was a large Christmas cracker also at each place, which the children wished to pull immediately, but they were told to wait until the pudding course. Another servant, this one also wearing a black dress (although it was a little shorter than that worn by her colleague), with a matching white cap and apron, came in carrying a silver tray on which were two bottles of wine, both of which had been opened. Mary Scott took charge of one of the bottles of Nederburg Sauvignon Blanc, while the servant went round the dining table pouring wine for those who wished it from the other one.

Alexander could remember that in Kenya there had been no maids, no female servants at all, apart from the *Ayah*, in any household he had known, and in their own home there had been a houseboy who served at mealtimes, who on grand occasions wore a white *kanzu* with a black sash wrapped around his waist, and a red fez on his head. In the kitchen the cook, known (as all cooks in East Africa were known) as *Mpishi*, which simply meant "Cook" in Swahili, was also male, as was the kitchen *toto*.

Mary Scott filled one of her three wine glasses and raised it to her lips, rapidly reducing the level by about an inch. She spoke to the maid, who returned shortly thereafter with a jug of orange juice for the children. There were already a number of jugs of water, along with some small bottles of carbonated apple juice, on the table, for those adults who did not wish to drink wine. Rory Maclean, Alexander's grandfather, declined a glass of wine, instead asking for a beer.

'I'ld like a beer too, if you don't mind, Mrs. Scott,' Mr. Oakley announced, as the maid was about to leave the room.

'Bring two beers, Dulcinella,' Mary Scott instructed the maid, who returned shortly thereafter with a pair of opened bottles of Castle lager, and two glasses, on a tray.

Alexander's Aunt Mary saw that everyone now had a glass either of wine, apple juice, water, orange juice or beer in front of them, and she raised her own glass of wine and wished her guests a happy Christmas. 'And a warm welcome to Africa to the Oakley family,' she added.

Mr. Oakley, the English guest, raised his beer and said 'Thank you. You have made my family feel very welcome, Mrs. Scott.'

'It takes getting used to, Christmas in high summer,' his wife commented at his side.

Alexander supped some of the cold *gazpacho* (although with some reservations), which was placed in front of him by one of the two maids, but he was not fond of seafood (other than the fish fingers with tomato sauce which his mother sometimes served for supper), and he, along with some of the other children, declined to eat the grilled *kabeljou* fillets which followed.

'This fish is delicious, Mary,' Alexander's father declared. 'What is it?'

Mary Scott smiled at her brother. '*Kabeljou.*' She pronounced it "cubblejoe." 'They were fresh from Hout Bay late yesterday afternoon, and I kept them on ice overnight.'

As each course was finished, the empty bowls and plates were removed by the two servants. Alexander's mother chatted with Mrs. Oakley, to whose somewhat anaemic features the wine had brought some colour, but Mr. Oakley applied himself silently to his meal and to his beer. Mary Scott had now finished her second glass of white wine. Alexander thoroughly approved of the roast turkeys, of which there were two giant birds, the first of which his grandfather, seated at the head of the long table, carved, and which were served with delicious golden baked potatoes, halved carrots and parsnips covered in honey and caramelized alongside the potatoes in the oven, fresh peas, baked onions, and pork, sage and onion stuffing.

One of the maids, instructed by Mary Scott, went and fetched a bottle of Constantia Pinot Noir. The wine had been uncorked.

'Turkey likes a red wine,' Mary Scott told her mother, who had stared as the bottle was placed on the table. Matching actions to words, Mary Scott offered her parents some of the red wine. When her offer was declined, she poured herself a glass. 'Who would like some red wine with their turkey?' she asked.

'I don't mind if I do,' declared Miss Spence-Traggart, presenting the second of the three wine glasses with which each place setting was furnished. Alexander's father took the old lady's glass which he filled from the bottle his sister handed him. He stood up and reached the glass across the table, and when Miss Spence-Traggart took it, he said 'Your good health!' and raised his own glass, which still held only white wine.

Some of the guests accepted second helpings of the turkey. By then Alexander's Aunt Mary was on her second glass of the Constantia red. In the kitchen earlier she had been sampling

54

the KWV brandy she had used in the preparation of the brandy butter which accompanied the Christmas pudding. Her manner had grown expansive, her speech just a little slurred. Alexander observed these phenomena without the least sense of judgement. Adults, and how they behaved, were often a mystery to him, a mystery he rarely sought to fathom. The big Christmas pudding, its surface flaring with tiny blue flames, was brought in by one of the maids. There were exclamations from the adults and cries of 'Ooh' from Alexander and the other children. The second maid brought two bottles of Robertson Winery sparkling wine on a tray, one of which Mary Scott directed be placed in front of her brother. 'Would you open it for us, Alex?' she asked him.

Alexander's father removed the foil around the cork and worked the cork up with his thumb, and there was a loud "pop!" followed by laughter as the sparkling wine under pressure began to spill from the bottle. Mrs. Maclean thrust her tall champagne flute (the third of the three wine glasses with which each place setting was furnished) at her husband, who caught the wine in the glass. 'Who else is for some bubbly?' he asked.

Mr. Oakley, along with the austere old gentleman resident, together with Alexander's grandparents and one of the old ladies, declined the offer. Alexander's father was busy for some minutes pouring the wine for the others.

Alexander thoroughly approved of the pudding, although his mother warned him not to eat too much. Alexander, such a skinny little boy, very particular about his food, could be surprisingly greedy with certain dishes, and he often found it difficult to exercise restraint when faced with sweet, gooey confections and plump, unctuous puddings. He found the brandy butter especially delicious. Mrs. Maclean watched him anxiously, and told him he had had enough after half a dozen heaped spoonfuls of pudding and a large helping of the brandy butter. 'I don't want you disgracing yourself later on, Sandy,' she said.

Two of the old ladies, and the austere old gentleman, along with Alexander's mother and father, his grandmother, and Aunty Mary herself, chose instead the fruit salad with ice cream, as did almost all the other children. Crackers were pulled. The two bottles of sparkling wine were emptied. The adults laughed at some of the silly jokes inside the crackers, and the children examined the novelties which fell out of them. Alexander and his cousin James both found clip-on moustaches, which they attached immediately, amidst laughter from the other children. Roy found a miniature spirit level inside his cracker, and he was very pleased with it, ascertaining whether the dining table surface was level. He said it was not.

Inside the old house it was pleasantly cool, but beyond the wide, covered veranda, the temperature in the shade had reached the upper eighties. Almost everyone at that Christmas lunch was of first, second or third generation British descent, and perhaps the sole concession made to the Cape Town midsummer heat had been the cold *gazpacho* soup. The lunch was otherwise not very different at all to the Christmas lunches being consumed that day in an England caught fast in the icy grip of midwinter. But all the boys, excepting only the little English boy (whose skin had not yet progressed beyond the burned red stage), had tans, and Alexander's and Roy's hair was bleached a pale gold by the sun.

Alexander did not feel very well after lunch. He found a wicker chair with a cushion in it at the far end of the long, deep veranda, away from the others, and sat back in the chair, folding his hands across his somewhat distended stomach. He closed his eyes and within five minutes he had fallen asleep.

Chapter Six

In late February of 1966 Alexander turned eleven. He had gone up a standard at school the month before, at the start of the new school year. He was almost overwhelmed by the birthday present he received from his parents: an inflatable dinghy, modelled on a life raft, which could contain three or four little boys comfortably, or one adult and two or three little boys with a bit of a squeeze. The mini life raft came equipped with a double-ended paddle and a foot operated pump with which to inflate it. January and February were Cape Town's warmest months. The temperature was to reach eighty-six degrees in the shade later that day. In the mid morning Alexander and his brother went outside and called for Simba, who appeared after a few minutes from the far side of the fence at the bottom of the garden. Roy scooped him up as the cat miaowed in his loud Siamese voice, and the two brothers took him inside the house. The windows were closed, and Simba was provided with a litter tray, water and some food. Dorcas was not working that particular Saturday morning.

'Have you both been to the lavatory recently?' Alexander's mother asked her sons. 'And you too, Stewart,' she said to the brothers' friend from across the road, who would be coming with them. Olivia Maclean had packed a picnic lunch in a wicker hamper. The family, accompanied by Stewart Fleming (who had given Alexander a book on trains for his birthday, chosen most likely by his mother; a thoughtful gift), piled into the Vauxhall, and they set off on the long drive for Boulders Beach, which was a short distance past Simon's Town. It would take well over an hour's driving to reach their destination.

Once they had reached Muizenberg the road hugged the shore, as did the Peninsula railway which connected Simon's Town, via Fish Hoek and other stops, with Cape Town city centre. Alexander always felt a thrill when a train passed by. Although now electrified, and lacking the excitement that a train pulled by a steam locomotive would have generated, Alexander still enjoyed seeing the heavy carriages go by, their wheels clackety-clacking over the joins in the rails. Sometimes passengers would wave back at the boy as he waved out the open window from the back seat. Alexander also anticipated with eagerness the coastal defence guns which they passed near the road shortly before reaching Simon's Town. During one drive, they had happened to pass one of these guns as it had fired a practice round, and Alexander had been thrilled almost witless for a while by the noise of the explosion he had heard, and by the heavy cloud of yellow-grey smoke which the gun's muzzle had produced. Thereafter, Alexander lived in hope during every journey past the guns of another live firing exercise taking place.

The old buildings, full of character and variety, in Simon's Town itself, which had been a Royal Navy base for many years, and was now the main base for the South African Navy, stirred Alexander's keenest interest. He enjoyed driving by Admiralty House as the road entered the town. The old house (which as it stood dated from the early nineteenth century), with its simple proportions and lack of excessive adornment, pleased Alexander's eye. It was a large but modestly styled, plastered and whitewashed double story building with a regular façade and evenly spaced windows, set only a little distance back from the road behind a stone wall, which was broken by a pair of massive, highly varnished wooden gates between tall, sturdy masonry pillars framed by Cape Dutch curliques, also plastered and whitewashed. Alexander knew that his great-grandfather, a captain in the Victorian navy, had for a while been based at Simon's Town, and he sometimes imagined his ancestor watching his descendant as the family drove slowly through the small naval town.

Boulders Beach was a broad cove of white sand bounded at either end by huge rounded rocks, and beyond the rocks at the far end of the beach was the penguin rookery, which was entirely overrun by Jackass penguins, which you could see at any time of the year. You could walk among the comical little creatures, and watch as they waddled down to the water's edge, then hurled themselves into the sea and within a moment, all their clumsiness gone, they had become creatures of grace and speed. The beach backed onto a narrow strip of land in front of a row of seaside villas, an area covered by low shrubs, amidst which the penguins bred and laid their eggs every year. In the shallow cove which visitors used as a bathing beach, Alexander, Roy and Stewart launched the mini life raft, having taken turns in working the foot pump to inflate it.

'Dont go far!' Alexander's mother told him. 'Dont go into deep water.'

False Bay was known for its sharks, among them the fearsome great white, yet neither of Alexander's parents, accustomed to Kenyan beaches protected by a coral reef some distance from the beach, which discouraged sharks from nearing bathers, mentioned this, and none of the boys gave it a moment's thought. Perhaps, as long as they stayed within the bounds of shallow water demarcated by promontories of huge boulders at either end of the beach, the likelihood of coming across a shark was slim. Certainly, neither then nor on subsequent visits to the beach with the life raft, did the children ever see any sharks. The boys all took turns using the double-ended paddle, and their happy chatter and laughter reassured Olivia Maclean that they were safe. Both Maclean brothers had learned to swim at the Kenya coast, and Stewart too knew how to swim, having learned during weekly summer visits to the swimming pool while at school.

After the blood warm waters of the Kenya coast, Alexander found bathing in the cold sea off the Peninsula coast far from pleasant. He rarely went into the water further than his knees if he could help it. Nor did he look forward to the weekly swimming outings at school. There was no swimming pool at Kromboom Park School. The children were bussed each week to Rondebosch Boys' Prep School, where they used that school's swimming pool. Sometimes Alexander felt so loath to get into the water, which he thought was icy cold, that he spent the hour lurking behind the changing rooms. On those occasions he was never missed.

The Macleans had supper at seven o' clock. During the summer it was still light after supper, and sometimes Alexander and Roy, occasionally joined by Stewart Fleming, would take their bikes and join up with two or three naughty boys they knew from school, who lived further down Mallaig Road, in the older section of the suburb, or up one of the streets which led off Mallaig Road. Jonathan Van der Walt, bigger and taller than Alexander, was a year ahead of Alexander at school, in standard five, and his family lived in a double story house with big trees in the garden, and they had a swimming pool. He was a bold, brash boy. Alexander knew that Gordon Cohen, another of these boys, was Jewish, but as he had no idea what a Jew was, nor that Jews should be treated in any way differently to other people, this meant nothing to him. The third boy, Robbie, was also in standard four, but not in the same class as Alexander.

The dusk was creeping in with sly speed across the roofs of the houses and settling in the streets. It was soon dark enough for the street lights to cast pools of warm light in the darkened street.

'Let's ring Mrs. Irwin's door bell,' Jonathan said.

Alexander did not think this was a good idea, but Robbie said 'Yeah!' so Alexander and Roy, along with Gordon, followed the other two boys down the street and into Golden Grove Road and they pulled up on their bikes a house short of old Mrs. Irwin's shabby house. Jonathan grinned and said 'Watch this!' and laying his bike on its side he opened Mrs. Irwin's front gate and walked silently up to her front door and rang her bell. Then he ducked behind a large shrub to one side of her *stoep*, and hid. After a minute had passed the front door opened and Mrs. Irwin peered out.

'Who's there?' she asked.

Robbie giggled, then put his hand over his mouth. Alexander hoped no one was watching them as they crouched behind the low garden wall of the house next door to Mrs. Irwin's, peering over the top of the wall.

'Who's there?' the old lady asked again, her voice quavering, and receiving no answer but a small movement in the shrubbery to the side of her *stoep*, she closed the door. After a few minutes Jonathan crept out from behind the shrubs and ran across the small lawn and vaulted over the low wall in front of Mrs. Irwin's property. He tried unsuccessfully to stifle his laughter with his hand. 'Ha ha!' he laughed. 'Now you have a go Robbie.'

And Robbie sneaked down the short pathway and up to Mrs. Irwin's front door, and rang the doorbell, then flung himself behind the shrubs to the side of the *stoep*. Again the front door was opened.

'Is anyone there?' Mrs. Irwin asked, her voice old and trembling. Silence held for half a minute, then she said 'If I see you, you bad boys, I'll tell your parents!' Then the poor old lady closed the front door again.

By Alexander's side Jonathan choked and spluttered as he tried not to laugh out loud, and after a little while, Robbie, who had very short, bristle-cut blonde hair, rejoined them, clambering easily over the low garden wall. As he did so, Alexander saw the curtains twitch in Mrs. Irwin's front room, and he knew that she would have seen the boy as he climbed over the wall, although she could not possibly have seen who he was in the dark.

The five boys crept back to their bikes lying on the grassy verge in front of the house next door to Mrs. Irwin's, and mounting them they freewheeled down the street back towards Mallaig Road. It was by now properly dark, and Alexander knew that he should not have stayed out so long after supper.

'Where have you been?' Mr. Maclean asked his sons as they entered via the kitchen door, having first put their bikes in the unused maid's room behind the garage, which had become a storage room. 'What have you been up to? It's getting late.'

'Nothing Dad,' Alexander replied. 'Just riding around with some of the boys.' But he felt ashamed, and he felt distress also, as if he was sharing in old Mrs. Irwin's upset and anxiety. These emotions hurt him. It was with difficulty that he met his mother's eye, and he knew that she must guess that he had been up to no good.

Soon after Alexander had turned eleven, his father had given him a slim volume titled "Sex Education for Boys". 'Perhaps this is a bit early,' his father said. 'I don't know. I don't want you feeling later on that Mum and I neglected this subject.'

Later, in the privacy of his own room, Alexander glanced through the book. It had hand-drawn illustrations. He did not think it was very interesting, but once in a while he would look at it. One afternoon, on a fine, clear day in May, at Jonathan's house, he sat in the tree house with Jonathan and Robbie. The leaves of the oak tree in which the tree house was built were taking on the colour of burnished bronze. The air had an autumnal tang to it. It was a wonderful day to be alive. Alexander's two school mates were discussing the reproductive aspects of sex, or rather, what they thought they knew about sex. Alexander realised that thanks to the book his father had given him, he knew more than either of them, about how babies were made.

'Lance jacks off,' Jonathan said, laughing. Alexander did not understand what Jonathan might mean by these words.

'Lance is a tosser!' Robbie replied. Jonathan and Robbie were both laughing now. But they soon lost interest in the topic, and Jonathan began to talk about the newly started rugby season. This subject did not interest Alexander at all, and he said 'I have to go now. I'll see you.'

'Bye Sandy,' the other two boys said, and Alexander climbed down from the tree house and grabbed his bike and pedalled the short distance home. The days of his innocence were not yet over.

Alexander, Roy and Stewart had used Mr. Maclean's *panga* to clear an area roughly twelve feet in diameter in the rather dense undergrowth between the fence at the back of the Maclean house and the Kromboom River. In it they had built a small shelter, a lean-to, having cut and trimmed some larger branches to build a framework which they bound with twine, over which they laid a mass of the slim, leafy, long stemmed plants which abounded in the location, and over this in turn they had stretched and fastened, using twine, an oblong of old canvas ground cloth which Stewart had filched from his father's garage. Often the three boys would meet there after school, and talk of many things: the things of everyday – movies they had seen recently at the drive-in cinema, or school gossip – and they would examine some of the unanswered questions in their lives, such as how old the music teacher's car was. Miss Armstrong (who was also Stewart's and Alexander's class teacher that year) drove a Humber Snipe, which was an ancient saloon car with dulled black paintwork, running boards, free-standing, nickel-plated headlights, and a tall, narrow, nickel-plated radiator grill. Stewart contended it had to be at least fifty years old, but Alexander had recently been looking through a collection of slim, illustrated volumes on car marques, which belonged to his father. They were published by Mobil Oil, and had always fascinated the brothers.

'I think her car is thirty years old at the oldest,' Alexander insisted. 'I think it was made just before the Second World War, which began in 1939. My Dad has some books on cars. I'll show you sometime.'

Stewart bowed to superior knowledge, and conceded that he may be wrong.

The boys then began to wonder how tall Table Mountain was. 'Thousands of feet,' Alexander said.

'Ten thousand,' Roy opined.

'I'll ask my Dad,' Stewart said. 'We went up once, in the cable car, and looked at the view. But I was still small, and I don't remember too well.'

'What did the top of the mountain look like?' asked Alexander.

'I think the mountain was bare on top,' Stewart replied, 'but my Dad said that there was forest further along, and dams with stone walls, and secret kloofs.'

'My Dad told Roy and me that we would go up one day, but I don't know when we will,' Alexander remarked, in wistful tones.

That evening, during supper, Alexander said to his father, 'Dad, when can we go to the top of Table Mountain?'

'Why don't we go up this weekend, Livia, if the weather is still OK?' Mr. Maclean asked his wife.

'I don't see why not. Let's do that.'

The fine autumn weather held, and Saturday dawned bright and still. There was a crispness to the air which stirred Alexander's blood, and held a promise of adventure and excitement. The boys wore pullovers and long trousers. 'It could be rather cold up there,' Mrs. Maclean pointed out. She prepared sandwiches and packed some peanut biscuits which Dorcas had made a day or two earlier, and some fruit, and a bottle of Ribena, already mixed, and a thermos of milky, sweetened coffee, and four crockery mugs wrapped in a couple of large dishcloths. All these she packed in a shoulder bag which Alexander's father would carry. The family set off at about ten in the morning, leaving Dorcas at work in the house. She would lock up when she left at noon, having first done her best to call Simba inside.

Once through Rondebosch town centre the family drove towards Cape Town along Rhodes Drive, a broad carriageway on the lower slopes of the mountain, high above Main Road. They passed the university on their left, laid out in ascending terraces on the mountainside, surely one of the most lovely university campus locations in the world. They also passed Mostert's Mill on their right, which Alexander always thought looked so interesting. It was a late 18th century wind powered corn mill with plastered, whitewashed walls, and it had huge wind vanes, the wooden frames painted green. Alexander would have liked to visit it one day, but he was never to do so, neither then, nor during later stays in Cape Town. The drive swept around the flanks of Devil's Peak, and below on the right lay District Six, a Cape Coloured high density residential neighbourhood, which had only within the last few months been declared a whites only area, and whose Coloured residents were to be cleared in 1968, and moved to townships located much further from the City, on the Cape Flats. As Alexander peered down the distant streets of District Six as they passed by above, with their double story commercial buildings and their tiny houses abutting right up against the pavements, he felt a sense of lives lived very differently to his own.

Once in the city centre, Alexander's father turned left into Kloof Nek Road, which climbed steadily towards the *nek* between Table Mountain and Lion's Head, and as they ascended, the old suburbs of Tamboerskloof lay on the right and Gardens to the left. But before the road began its descent to Clifton and Camps Bay, on the Atlantic shores of the Peninsula (with Lion's Head, the smaller of the two peaks which framed Table Mountain, looming behind them), the family turned left into Tafelberg Road, which followed a contour flanking Table Mountain's face. The lower cable station was located some distance along this road. At the cable station they parked the car.

Alexander and Roy were tremendously excited, watching as the downward gondola approached them, ever so slowly at first, then seemingly, faster and faster, and after it had docked, and the few passengers had got out, the Macleans, along with a number of other passengers, entered it. The gondola was tiny, about five feet wide and ten feet long. There was a narrow bench either side. The attendant closed and locked the car's entrance gate and the contraption took off with a sudden jerk, which set it rocking for a minute or two, forward and aft. The boys and Mrs. Maclean gasped. They left behind the cable station structure, and suddenly it felt as if they were floating free. At first it did not seem very far to the ground below, although the ground fell rapidly further and further away, but then the sandstone face of Table Mountain began to draw rapidly closer, and closer still, and it seemed to Alexander that they were going to collide with the vertical face of unyielding rock, but seemingly at the last possible moment the gondola began to climb steeply upwards.

The view behind them, and to their right, grew more and more impressive. Alexander looked out the back of the car: the city of Cape Town lay spread out like a toy town, and in the docks, alongside the quays, were rendered in miniature a dozen or more big ships, including a passenger liner, and many smaller vessels. Far offshore there were ships rounding the Cape of Good Hope, steaming both eastward and westward, following the sea lane around what Alexander thought of as the utmost southern point of Africa. He turned his eyes back to the mountain, and was surprised to see how fast they were approaching the top of the sheer ascent of rock. The gondola began to slow before entering the narrow docking bay in the cavernous concrete upper cable station, where the noise of the winding motors was magnified, echoing and rumbling, and the car came to a sudden, jerky halt, and rocked a few times, then was still. An attendant unlocked the car's gate, and the passengers, most of them talking loudly and excitedly, as if they had survived some natural disaster, climbed some stairs and found themselves suddenly in bright sunlight, on hard, bare, rocky ground, more than three thousand five hundred feet above sea level.

Alexander and Roy rushed off at a mad run, yelling and jumping. 'We're on top of the world!' Alexander shouted in his high, pure treble.

'We can touch the sky!' Roy cried, flinging his arms up towards the clean blue heavens, in which there was not a cloud to be seen.

'Boys!' shouted Alexander's father, 'Dont go near the edge!'

Alexander slowed his mad dash and looked around him properly. He saw a lovely little building of cut and dressed stone ahead of him, with high stepped gables, large bay windows at the two nearest corners, and a pair of sturdy chimneys. 'What is that building, Dad?' he asked.

Alexander's father smiled. 'That's the restaurant. We wont be visiting it this time, as I'm carrying our lunch with us.' He patted the bag he had slung over one shoulder.

The family descended to the viewing terrace below the restaurant, from which they could make out the suburbs of Clifton and Camps Bay far below, on the lower slopes of the mountainside, edged with beaches of white sand that Alexander had never visited. They could see the diminishing peaks of the Twelve Apostles marching to the south. To their right, but some distance below their present height, they saw Lion's Head rising like a conical sugar loaf, the white painted surveyor's beacon at the peak clearly visible, and beyond it lay Lion's Rump and Signal Hill.

After a while the family left the cable station behind them, following a track which led them along the length of the Front Table. They walked for about twenty minutes, the boys dashing ahead and running in circles like excited dogs. Far to the north-east was the great barrier of mountains that guarded Africa's hinterland. To the north-west the coastline extended into a distant haze. Their view of the great sweep of False Bay was almost entirely obscured by the near ground, but they could see the mountain ranges on the far side of the bay. There was an indication of the range of mountains that marched down the Peninsula's spine, and at one point, as they walked, Alexander thought he could make out forests atop the mountain to the south. The sensations of elevation and of clarity of light were intoxicating. The surface underfoot was hard and stony, with some low scrub growing amidst the rocks, which had yellow and grey lichen growing on them.

The family reached the head of a great cleft in the rock. This was the top of Platteklip Gorge, the steep, challenging route to the top of the mountain which the earliest explorers had taken. There were less challenging routes via the Back Table (Alexander was to become familiar with them all as a very young man), but during the early years of exploration and settlement the mountain would have been protected by dense forest and fierce beasts on that approach.

The brothers rushed forward to the edge of this great cleft in the face of the mountain, and Mr. Maclean shouted 'Stay away from the edge!' But he did not go forward to shepherd the boys back to safer ground. He was mortally afraid of heights, and he dared not go where they had gone.

'Alexander – Roy! Come here now!' their father called, a note of anxiety in his voice. Reluctantly, the two Maclean brothers stepped back from the edge of the mountain, and Mr. Maclean breathed an audible sigh of relief.

The group sat on a flat topped rock far enough back from the abyss to please Mr. Maclean. They had magnificent views of Cape Town and Table Bay below them, laid out like an architect's or urban planner's model. They ate their sandwiches and drank their Ribena or their coffee.

'Look Dad. There's an island far out in the sea!' Alexander said.

'That's Robben Island. It's a prison island,' Alexander's father replied. The island, which would become notorious in years to come, lay surprisingly far from the shore.

Afterwards the family walked further along the table top, but after a while they decided to turn around, although still some distance short of Maclear's Beacon at the far end of the table top.

Alexander was entranced and excited at the same time by the mountain top. He had rarely felt such an excess of delight and energy and wellbeing. He stopped and stared around him repeatedly: at the ranges of even mightier mountains far to the north-east, at the Peninsula mountain chain as it receded towards Cape Point to the south, and at the ships in Cape Town harbour, so tiny as to be like a fleet of toy ships. The family having returned to the viewing terrace near the restaurant (whose lavatories both brothers, along with their father, had had to use), Alexander gazed out across the sea towards an horizon which seemed unbelievably distant: there was a clean line, slightly but noticeably curved, where darker aquamarine met the lighter azure of the sky. It was at this time, aged eleven years, that Alexander's love of mountains and of the high places in the natural world was born. It was a love which was to be many times indulged when he reached manhood.

Chapter Seven

The Macleans were not great churchgoers. But once every four or five weeks, Mr. Maclean, moved by memories of his own childhood, conceived of the wish to attend a Sunday church service. Then the family would drive either to the Rondebosch Presbyterian Church, past Rondebosch Common, or to Saint Paul's Anglican Church in the centre of Rondebosch. Both were substantial buildings, the former in a more modern idiom, but Saint Paul's (so Alexander thought) was the more attractive of the two churches, built as it was of dressed stone, with stained glass windows. Alexander's father was more comfortable in the Presbyterian Church, as his family had belonged to the Church of Scotland during his childhood, but Olivia Maclean preferred attending a service at Saint Paul's, as she was, if anything, a member of the Church of England. So they compromised, alternating their attendance between the two churches.

Neither Alexander nor his brother Roy had ever attended Sunday school. In this they were in a minority among the children in their neighbourhood. Their only regular exposure to the Bible was during weekly religious instruction classes at school. Alexander however, who read much more than Roy, was familiar with the better known stories from the Bible through his reading of Arthur Mee's *Children's Bible*. Aged eleven, he had neither familiarity with nor the least understanding of the fundamental beliefs of the Christian faith: that Jesus Christ died that our sins might be forgiven us, and that He rose from the dead that we might know eternal life. In this Alexander was no different to most children his age. He found the services in the Presbyterian Church sombre and dull, and many of the hymn tunes were, he thought, difficult to sing. During the long hot summer months, the air inside the Presbyterian church building in particular was as warm and heavy as a thick blanket, so he sometimes dozed off during the main sermon. The Anglican services appealed to him much more: the priest in his colourful vestments seemed a far more impressive figure, yet also more approachable, than the Presbyterian minister in his austere black gown. He was attracted to the Anglican Church's high ritual, which included the presence of altar boys and choir boys wearing red cassocks and white surplices, and he enjoyed the hymn singing. The Anglicans, he thought, had better tunes than the Presbyterians. Nor was the Anglican priest's sermon ever as lengthy as the main sermon he had to sit through in the Presbyterian Church.

Perhaps the foundations of faith were being laid during these Sunday church outings. If so, Roy was never to build on them, but Alexander was to come to a sudden religious awakening aged seventeen, during his final year at school. But for now, both he and his brother found these outings more of a mild nuisance than anything else. There were better ways, they both felt, to spend a precious Sunday morning that sitting inside a church. However, almost all the children they knew in the neighbourhood would be doing likewise on a Sunday morning.

Mr. Maclean addressed the Anglican minister as "Padre," after the service, as the minister stood at the door greeting his parishioners and shaking their hands. The Presbyterian minister he addressed as "Reverend."

'Does our parish secretary have your names and address?' the Anglican minister asked Mr. Maclean, after their second visit to Saint Paul's. 'No?' He called a middle aged woman over, who was standing chatting to a small group nearby. 'Mrs. Fonteyn, Mr. and Mrs. Maclean moved to Cape Town recently from Kenya. Perhaps you would be sure to obtain their contact details?'

And so the Macleans were entered as parishioners at Saint Paul's, and one evening the Anglican minister visited the Macleans at home, staying for a sherry. Other than responding to his greetings, neither Alexander nor Roy said a word during his visit, although they remained in the sitting room throughout. Mr. Maclean, who enjoyed a social occasion, made the minister very welcome, and tried to press a second glass of sherry upon him, but the Reverend Michael Carrington declined the offer, pleading another engagement.

The Presbyterian minister, a younger man, called one Saturday afternoon. He had a Scottish name, Thomas Fraser. He and Mr. Maclean got on very well together, and Mrs. Maclean, as was often the case on a social occasion, allowed her husband to take the lead in the conversation. It was not that Mrs. Maclean was shy, so much as quiet and thoughtful.

Once in a while Mr. and Mrs. Fleming from across the road came to afternoon tea during the weekend. Then Alexander's mother would have made sure that Dorcas had baked a cake.

'This cake is delicious, Olivia,' Mrs. Fleming commented. 'You must give me the recipe.'

Alexander's mother smiled. 'I'll write it down for you,' she replied. Dorcas would give it to her.

Mr. Fleming was a quiet man, and his wife did almost all the talking. This she did in her affected tones, and Alexander thought her voice was rather grating. She would always have Stewart's little sister, Annie, with her. The child was as round as a dumpling, and would sit and scoff cake, and Alexander watched as cake and icing were smeared all around the child's rosebud mouth and plump chin and rosy cheeks. Then he would begin to feel a little queasy, and put his own slice of cake down. Stewart did not usually accompany his family to these tea parties.

Alexander had something of his father's volubility in him when the mood took him. Mr. Fleming sat listening as Alexander described how pretty the little stone restaurant on top of Table Mountain was.

'Are you interested in buildings?' Mr. Fleming asked him.

'Yes, I am, Mr. Fleming. I like to see how they're built. Stone buildings are my favourite.'

'Mine also,' Mr. Fleming responded. 'When I designed our house, I wished to incorporate stone in the finish. You've seen our fireplace, have n't you?'

'Yes, Mr. Fleming. I like it.'

The fireplace in the Fleming home was done in dressed stone.

'Would you like to be an architect when you grow up?'

'Or maybe go to sea,' Alexander replied. 'I like ships, Mr. Fleming.'

The company was listening to this rare exchange, rare because Mr. Fleming usually had so little to say.

'You'll need a good pass in Maths for both,' Mr. Fleming continued. And Alexander felt a moment's disquiet, for Maths was not a subject at which he excelled at school.

'Perhaps I'll have my own yacht,' he responded.

Mrs. Fleming laughed. 'That would be a fine thing!' she declared, in a tone which indicated that she thought this was very unlikely. In this she was wrong: Alexander would one day own a small yacht. Some dreams do come true.

When Alexander's parents went out in the evening (something they did not do very often, but occasionally they were invited out to dinner, or they had to attend some function organised by the oil company Mr. Maclean worked for), they turned to a friend from Kenya days, Bob Fletcher, who now lived in Cape Town, to babysit for them. The Maclean brothers liked Bob immensely. He was a bachelor, and fun, and unlike most grownups, he did not talk down to the boys, but treated them as rational and intelligent beings.

'Aha! I see your Mum and Dad have left the bottle of scotch out for me,' Bob declared, after saying goodbye to Alexander and Olivia Maclean as they left for the evening. Alexander's parents had left a plate of ham and cheese sandwiches, and a bottle of scotch with a whiskey tumbler alongside it, on the coffee table in the sitting room.

'But they've marked it with pencil, Uncle Bob,' Alexander said. 'Look!' He showed Bob Fletcher the marks drawn by his father on the whiskey label, which permitted their babysitter three generous tots of whiskey – and no more.

Bob laughed. 'They're *kali* people, your Mum and Dad! OK – I tell you what, let's make me a coffee first. Do you lads know how to make a coffee?'

'Oh no, Uncle Bob, Dorcas or Mummy makes the coffee.'

'Well then, let's go through to the kitchen. I'm sure we can find what we need,' and the three people, one a tall, lanky young man with short brown hair, wearing a sports jacket, and the others two very blonde headed little boys, went to the kitchen, where between the three of them they found where the instant coffee was kept, and the milk in the GEC fridge, and the sugar, and they boiled some water and made Bob Fletcher's coffee in a mug with a picture of a vintage motor car on it.

'Can I carry it to the sitting room?' asked Roy.

'It's a bit too full, I think. I'd better do it this time, Roy,' their honorary uncle answered him. In the sitting room Bob drank some of the coffee, then he took the bottle of scotch and poured a little whiskey into the mug, and said 'Can one of you lads go fetch me a teaspoon please?'

Roy ran to the kitchen and returned with a teaspoon, with which Bob Fletcher stirred the whiskey-invigorated coffee. He sucked the teaspoon and wiped it on his shirt front, then put it on the coffee table. 'Would you chaps like a story?' he asked.

'Oh yes please!' both boys replied.

'Ok, I'll tell you about the time I was in the water with a croc …' and their babysitter commenced a story about a boat he had been motoring in on Lake Victoria, whose prop had become fouled with water weed, and how he had had to remove his shirt and jump over the side with a knife and try to cut the weeds free, and how he had had to duck his head beneath the murky brown water, and how when he raised his head, the passengers had been shouting and pointing, and he had turned his head, 'and there was a huge croc surging through the water at me, determined to have me for lunch.'

The boys, one on either side of him on the sofa, stared at Bob Fletcher with big round eyes, and when he was finished telling the story, they thought it was a very fine one, and both said 'Tell us another story, please Uncle Bob!'

So their babysitter drank some more of the coffee laced with scotch whiskey, and said 'Right-o. What about the time my aunt, visiting from England, had to share the lavatory with a large iguana?'

Alexander laughed at the image that came to mind. 'Tell us the story!' he cried.

'Well, it was like this …' began Bob Fletcher.

With the coming of the cold, wet winter months, Alexander fell ill twice, running a temperature and being confined to bed each time. He felt profoundly miserable and horribly unwell. His asthma returned each time, and he longed for his mother's comforting presence when she was not in the room. Olivia Maclean spent as much time as she could with her eldest son during these illnesses, sitting reading, or knitting, in a chair alongside his bed, while Dorcas got on with the housework during the day. But in the evenings, Alexander's father returned from work, and his mother had to leave her son alone for longer periods while she prepared the family's supper. Alexander's father looked in on his son a few times, staying with him for a short while each time, but like many men, he was not totally at ease during a visit to a sick bed, and Alexander could sense this.

Yet these were but brief periods of sickness during the three and a half months of winter, and there were quite a few days through the winter when the weather was perfect, and the sun shone from a clear sky, and the day was still. Then, if the good weather happened to fall on a weekend, the Maclean family would pile into the car and drive somewhere. Often, Stewart Fleming would accompany them. Alexander cherished his friend's company, and having Stewart along made a family outing seem extra special for him. One Saturday afternoon that winter, the sun shining, the Macleans, together with Stewart, drove into the city centre, and parked the car in Wale Street, and walked the short distance to the Gardens, Cape Town city centre's large public park, located on the original site of the VOC (Dutch East Indies Company) produce gardens. There were beautifully tended lawns as smooth and flawless as the baize on a billiard table, behind low, decorative, painted metal barriers over which you could easily step, but which were placed as a psychological barrier to prevent the grass being worn to dirt by visitors. The flower beds were still full of cannas and hibiscus, and there were rose bushes on which there were still some blooms making a brave show. The park was planted with mature trees, among which the oak trees, so iconic of the Western Cape, were prominent. They were leafless now, the skeletal framework of their branches portraying the very essence of a tree. There were grey squirrels loping fluidly across the lawns and grubbing in the short grass beneath the trees, still hoping to find some overlooked acorns. The little creatures, which delighted the children, were rarely still for long, and were almost tame, having been accustomed for generations to being fed by visitors.

'Oh Dad! Can we buy some peanuts for the squirrels?' Alexander begged his father. Mr. Maclean bought the three boys a bag of peanuts each, and the children soon had a crowd of squirrels mobbing them for the tasty treats. The children's laughter was a happy sound, and Mr. and Mrs. Maclean were both smiling.

There was a tearoom in the park, with wrought iron tables and chairs arranged beneath the wintry trees. Here the Maclean family and their guest took a break after walking around the park for about twenty minutes. Alexander's parents ordered a coffee and a slice of cake each, while the children were bought milkshakes and little jam filled donuts, which left their fingers and their mouths jammy and sticky. Mrs. Maclean passed around some paper serviettes from the chromed metal dispenser which sat on the table. 'Here,' she said, 'lick your fingers and wipe your mouths.'

Alexander caught Stewart's friendly green eyed gaze. Stewart smiled at Alexander, who smiled happily back at him.

On one occasion the Italian teenager from next door, the leggy, raven haired Paola, accompanied the Macleans on an outing to Kirstenbosch Gardens. Roy was almost overwhelmed by her presence, and Alexander was happy also. The group walked slowly up the path through the gardens which led to the Smuts Track, which climbed to the Back Table via Skeleton Gorge. They ascended as far as the Contour Path – quite a trek – the trail which followed a contour line along the flanks of the mountain at a height of about one thousand three hundred feet above sea level. Here, where the Smuts Track crossed the Contour Path, they found themselves beneath a canopy of indigenous trees, which included yellowwoods (although the mighty yellowwoods the early settlers in the Cape had found on the mountain slopes were long gone now, turned into roof beams and floor planking and furniture in the oldest buildings in Cape Town), along with *Kiggelaria Africana*, somewhat incorrectly known as the wild peach, ironwood, *rooiels*, and assegai trees. Alexander was delighted to see how the stream coming down the gorge broadened into a calm, shallow, shaded pool about fifteen feet across. The proximity of water always brought Alexander pleasure. The family, with their pretty young guest, spent half an hour at this picturesque location, the adults sitting on a fallen tree trunk, the children, yelling with excitement and high spirits, running some distance along the Contour Path in either direction, and also some way up Skeleton Gorge. When free of asthma, Alexander was as fit and as full of energy as any other eleven year old boy.

One Sunday afternoon, during a cold front which had been sitting atop Cape Town and the Peninsula like a cold wet eiderdown for a week or more, the Macleans, on their way back from Alexander's grandparents at Kommetjie, whom they had left somewhat earlier than usual, turned off Rhodes Drive, having driven into thick mist as they crested the pass at Constantia Nek, and pulled up outside Hohenstein. The house was rendered evanescent by heavy mist (or perhaps it was low lying cloud?) but from higher up the slope Alexander had seen some of its chimneys, as if disembodied, showing through the mist. Alexander gazed at the scene, captivated by the sight of this grand old house high up in the clouds on the side of the mountain, and he found himself wishing, as he often did, that he lived here. When they got out of the car he could smell the scent of resinous pine trees in the cold damp air. Alexander's Aunt Mary was seated in the great hall, in a tall wing chair upholstered in plum coloured brocade, along with Miss Spence-Traggart and Miss Grohen. There was a half-empty bottle of white wine on the small table, and three glasses, along with a small hand bell, with which to summon a servant. A large fire crackled and hissed in the huge fireplace, and the vast room was scented with burning pine and Cyprus wood, heady and aromatic.

'Brother of mine!' Alexander's aunt cried. 'Olivia – and the boys! Welcome! What will you have to drink? We're having drinky-poos early, it seems the thing to do in this weather.'

Mary Scott kissed her brother and Olivia, and smiled at her nephews. The Misses Spence-Traggart and Grohen inclined their heads graciously to the newcomers.

'Where are James and Tom, Aunty Mary?' asked Alexander.

'Oh – the lads are somewhere in the house. Perhaps in their room? Why don't you go up and see if you can find them?'

Alexander and Roy dashed back through the entrance hall, via which the Macleans had reached the great hall. They scampered up the wide staircase, which opened off the entrance hall. Then they took the next, rather narrower flight of stairs, reaching the second floor, where their cousins shared a large room at one end of the house. Here they found James sitting in a chair reading a book, while his younger brother, Tom, played with toy soldiers on the worn and somewhat threadbare Persian rug in front of the fireplace. There was no fire burning in the grate, but a small electric incandescent heater gave off a warm double glow. The elderly spaniel was asleep on the rug in front of this electric heater. There was a distinct odour of warm, unwashed dog in the room. James looked up.

'Hullo James,' Alexander greeted him. Only the English guest, Mr. Oakley, who was by now long gone, had addressed James by anything other than his full Christian name. It should have been clear to him that James had not enjoyed being called 'Jim,' but Mr. Oakley had not appeared to notice.

James put his book down. 'Hey – Sandy, Roy! How are you guys?'

Tom turned his head and looked up. 'Do you want to play soldiers with me?' he asked his visiting cousins. Roy knelt down next to his younger cousin.

'What are you reading?' Alexander asked James.

'*Swallows and Amazons*.'

'Oh – that's a good story. I wish I could have a small sailing dinghy. Dad says when I'm older, I can join the sailing club on Zeekoei Vlei. Is it your own book, or from the library?'

'Mum bought it for me. Shall we go outside and see how high the stream is?'

'Yeah – let's do that.'

Roy stayed inside with Tom. He had taken one of the two opposing armies, and the two boys had begun a battle using a pair of dice, and adhering to complicated rules, which Tom, who had devised the game, was explaining to Roy. But James and Alexander ran downstairs, and grabbing their coats in the hallway, they ran through the great hall and out onto the veranda. As they passed by, Mrs. Maclean called 'Where are you going, Sandy?'

'To look at the stream, Mum.'

'Alright. Dont fall in.' The boys, who had been joined by the German shepherd dog, ran across the lawn towards the forest of pine and oak trees.

A mountain-fed stream ran down the side of the property, and during these winter months, it assumed sizable proportions. Alexander gazed with fascination at the torrent. The stream had burst its banks and was flooding over the ground beneath the old oak trees. He picked up a stick and threw it in the water. James followed suit. The two boys watched their sticks racing down the flood of water.

'Bet mine reaches the bridge first,' said James.

'No ways! Watch my stick go!'

There was a little wooden bridge which usually crossed the stream and carried the path on through the woods. Both ends of the bridge were flooded now. The sticks hurried towards the structure, the boys running along the edge of the floodline. Then the dog jumped into the water and retrieved James' stick, bringing it to him. The dog shook itself violently and water flew high into the air. Both boys laughed and danced out of the way. The dog barked excitedly.

When they returned to the house, the dog settling on its bed in the great hall again, it was to find a huge, partially demolished walnut cake on the table, with a now near empty bottle of wine alongside it, and a scattering of tea cups, along with a tea pot, a milk jug and a sugar basin. Miss Spence-Traggart and Miss Grohen, who were still holding their wine glasses in their hands, both had hectic spots of high colour showing on their cheeks beneath the powder. Alexander's parents had been drinking tea. Both boys halted.

'Can we have some cake please, Mum?' asked James.

'Of course you may.'

Alexander was very fond of walnut cake. He was pleased to see how big the slice his aunt gave him was. He found an empty chair nearby and began to shovel the cake into his mouth, his gluttonous pleasure in the sweet, rich comestible and the crisp walnuts quite overcoming him. It did not take him long to finish eating the slice of cake. His aunt, who had poured the last of the wine into her glass, said 'Have another slice, Sandy,' and thrust a second, equally large slice of cake towards him.

'You'll spoil your supper, Sandy,' his mother told him. 'Just have half of that. Here – let me cut it.'

Alexander allowed his mother to cut the slice of cake in half, then he ate the half she returned to him. The other half his mother herself ate.

When the Macleans at last got home, it was growing dark. It had begun raining again. Simba greeted the family with indignant yowls at having been left alone so long. Alexander and Roy made a fuss of the cat.

'Shall we have our drinky-poos?' Alexander's mother asked her husband. Mr. Maclean laughed.

'I'll have a coffee if I may, Darling,' he said.

'And then I must do something about supper – if we've got any room left for supper after that gigantic walnut cake.'

'Mary always has believed in feeding the inner man,' Mr. Maclean commented.

Chapter Eight

The Macleans only rarely went to the cinema. Cape Town then had dozens of suburban cinema houses. Perhaps the most convenient one to reach from the Macleans' home was the Scala Cinema, on Main Road in Claremont. In late winter one Saturday afternoon the brothers' parents took them to a matinée screening at the Scala to watch *The Great Race*, starring Jack Lemmon, Tony Curtis and Natalie Wood. Such an outing was a great treat for the brothers, and Alexander's excitement and anticipation were shared by Roy. The foyer, with its painted *faux* marble finish on the walls, was crowded, and was scented with hot popcorn. It was noisy also, everyone talking at once. The five minute foyer bell sounded soon after the Macleans arrived, and they entered the auditorium, where an usherette wearing a pillbox hat, carrying a small torch in one hand, took their tickets and directed them to their seats. They were about ten rows back from the screen.

The boys' anticipation mounted as the lights were dimmed, and they watched the variety of local handmade commercials which followed uncritically, according to each an equal degree of attention. They laughed loudly at the Looney Tunes animated cartoon which flickered onto the screen after the commercials.

Oh – Elmer Fudd was such a solemn, silly, pompous little chap! And Bugs Bunny, his nemesis, was such a laid back bunny. A Walt Disney cartoon followed, which Alexander did not think was as funny as the Looney Tunes cartoon which had preceded it. Then there followed an interval, and the house lights were turned up, and the erstwhile usherettes in their pillbox hats, now carrying trays suspended in front of them from straps over their shoulders, and stacked with ice cream tubs, chocolate bars, small containers of popcorn, and cold drinks, paraded up and down the aisles.

'Would you boys like some popcorn?' their father asked them.

'Yes please!' they chorused. Their father raised an arm and clicked his fingers, and called 'Miss!' and one of the young women approached the end of the row in which they were seated.

'Two popcorns please,' Mr. Maclean called, and he stood and made his way crab-wise past his neighbours' knees to the end of the row, where he handed the young woman a one Rand note, for which he received change. The popcorn smelled salty and slightly oily, and was just what Alexander now thought he needed, although minutes earlier a chocolate might have been preferable. Then the foyer bell buzzed again, and shortly thereafter the lights were dimmed, and the main feature commenced.

The Great Race was a fine Technicolor comedy-melodrama, in which the vintage cars, which the boys liked very much, were as important as the actors. The boys laughed so much at the ridiculous situations the characters kept finding themselves in, they almost lost their breath, and their father roared with laughter too, but there was also plenty of high drama, and the exotic settings were magnificent. Alexander thought it was a wonderful movie.

'So,' their father asked them as they left the cinema and found themselves, somewhat disconcertingly, in the gathering dusk of a wintry early evening, 'did you chaps enjoy that?'

'It was lovely, Daddy,' Alexander replied.

'I thought it was the best film I've ever seen,' Roy told his parents.

'What did you think, Livia?' Mr. Maclean asked his wife.

'Yes, it was n't bad. There were plenty of vintage cars for you boys, were n't there?'

'Thanks for taking us, Mum and Dad,' Alexander said. 'I wish we could see it again.'

Within a few days of the visit to the cinema, first Alexander, then his brother, contracted chicken pox. Oh, what a beastly illness it was! Not only was there the fever each boy ran (in Alexander's case, he had a temperature of just over 101), but there were the foul itchy sores, which wept fluid and eventually scabbed over. The most difficult of these itchy sores for Alexander to cope with were those in his anus: they drove him almost frantic for a while. The first that Alexander's mother knew of her son's affliction was when she noticed him scratching himself repeatedly during the course of one afternoon, on the tummy and the back, struggling to reach round behind him. She made him remove his pullover and shirt and vest, and although she had n't seen chicken pox since her own childhood, she guessed what the small itchy red spots which looked like insect bites meant, for although both the boys had already had mumps before leaving Kenya, neither of her sons had yet had chicken pox. This diagnosis was confirmed by the doctor when he paid a call to the Maclean household.

'I would imagine that both you and your husband have had chicken pox as children. But Roy is sure to catch it; it is a highly contagious disease.'

'Yes, we both had chicken pox during childhood. How long does it last, Doctor?'

'Not long, about a week. Your sons will run a temperature. Treat the fever with acetaminophen, such as Tylenol. Do not give them aspirin.'

'What can I do to relieve their itching?'

'Give your sons a colloidal oatmeal bath in lukewarm water every four or five hours, then pat them dry, and apply calamine lotion to their skin. I'll prescribe an ointment which can be applied in the anus. You can obtain calamine lotion and an oatmeal preparation at the pharmacy.'

Mrs. Maclean left the suffering Alexander, and his as yet unafflicted brother, in Dorcas' kindly and sympathetic care while she took the car and drove into Rondebosch town centre to visit the chemist. Dorcas had children of her own, not all of whom had yet had chicken pox, but neither woman seemed overly concerned that Dorcas, being in close proximity to Alexander (and within days, Roy also), would bring the disease into her own home.

Alexander and Roy came to anticipate the oatmeal baths with great eagerness, for the relief these brought them. In between these baths, they felt irritable and unhappy, and at night they slept badly. Their mother suffered vicariously, hating to see her children so unhappy. But within just over a week, Alexander's itchy sores had disappeared, along with his fever, and Roy too experienced a great improvement in his situation a few days later.

In September, with the coming of spring, Stewart told Alexander that his father had to visit Durban on a business trip.

'How long will he be away?' Alexander asked.

'I think just a few days,' Stewart replied. 'We're going to drive my Dad to the airport tomorrow afternoon.'

Alexander saw the entire Fleming family leaving in their Volvo at about four o' clock the next afternoon. He overheard his mother talking to his father that evening.

'There's a possibility the Flemings may be moving to Durban. Something about opening a new office there.'

'But I don't want Stewart to leave,' Alexander thought.

'Do you know why your Dad's gone to Durban?' Alexander asked Stewart after school the next day.

'I'm not sure,' Stewart replied.

Alexander hoped very much that it was not true, that the Flemings might not after all be going away any time in the future.

Meanwhile, Alexander's father and mother had been out to dinner with people whose name, Fellbridge, Alexander could not remember having heard before. Bob Fletcher had come round to babysit the brothers that evening.

One evening not long thereafter, Alexander , who was lurking just beyond the kitchen door again, overheard his mother say to his father, as she was preparing the supper in the kitchen 'It just seems such a risk, Alex. We're doing alright now, are n't we?'

Alexander missed what his father said in reply, except the words '… do much better if I go in with Graham on this venture.'

'… our entire savings …' Alexander's mother responded. 'And uprooting the boys.'

Alexander was as still as a mouse just along the corridor from the kitchen. He knew that he should not listen to other people's private conversations, but in this case he felt it was important that he did so. But all he caught from his father were the words '… spirit of adventure.'

Then Alexander went through to the sitting room, and picked up the book he had been reading earlier. Shortly thereafter his father entered the sitting room, carrying a glass of beer. He sat down and reached for the Argus. It was to be another ten years before television was introduced in South Africa. The wireless (as the Macleans still called it, unless they were referring to Mrs. Maclean's transistor radio, which lived in the kitchen) played a much greater part in their lives than it was to do in later years. Mr. Maclean was very proud of his big PYE radiogram, a beautifully made piece of furniture of polished hardwood, with a closely woven off-cream coloured raffia facing behind which were the speakers. To operate the radiogram you opened the polished wooden front cover above the raffia facing, and the wireless controls were then revealed, as was the gramophone player on the right hand side.

Mr. Maclean had a small collection of long playing records, of which the *Inkspots* (an American Negro crooners' group popular in the 1940s and 1950s), and *A Swinging Safari* (an instrumental composition by Bert Kaemfert and his Orchestra, released in early 1962 and very popular among ex-Kenyans), were (together with a collection of songs by the American *basso profundo* Negro singer Paul Robeson), among his favourites.

'Let's listen to the *Inkspots*,' Alexander's father said.

'Oh yes, shall I put the record on, Dad?' Alexander responded.

'Yes please, Sandy,' his father replied.

Alexander opened the unit, pressed the "On" button, and turned the selector to "Gramophone." Then he removed the LP carefully from its sleeve, and placed it on the turntable. He checked that the turntable speed was set at 33, and not at 45. Then he pushed the "Play" lever across with his thumb, and with a series of clicks, the arm with the needle at its tip raised itself, moved across, and lowered the needle onto the edge of the recording spiral.

'Turn it up a little, Sandy,' his father asked him, so Alexander turned the volume control up a notch.

'I don't want to set the World on fire ...' Alexander crooned, accompanying the singer. His father watched him, smiling.

Sometimes, generally on a weekend, Alexander went riding. He enjoyed being around horses. He was always pleased when Aunty Margaret (as she did the following Sunday during the Macleans' visit to his grandparents in Kommetjie) took him to the livery stables in Noordhoek where she kept her two horses, a *Haflinger* gelding of fourteen hands, and a *Boerperd* mare of sixteen hands. The livery was a small one, stabling only eight horses, and comprised a row of loose boxes in an old, low, plastered and whitewashed building with a thatched roof, which stood amidst oak and pine trees. There were two big meadows with rich grass in which wildflowers bloomed, and a jumble of tack rooms and harness rooms, along with a large wooden shed for feed. These stables were just one of many in Noordhoek, a district well known for horses.

The *Haflinger* gelding, with its light chestnut coat and biscuit coloured mane and tail, was a very pretty horse. The mare was a chestnut with a white blaze and white stockings. When Alexander rode, he always rode Johnny, the *Haflinger* gelding, partly because it was the smaller of the two animals, and partly because it had the more gentle nature. Alexander was tall enough now to saddle Johnny up for himself, although he had to strain to reach the saddle up onto the horse's back, and he could fix the bit and bridle in place, and he would curry-comb his mount vigorously after a ride, and check inside Johnny's hoofs for dried, crusted mud, and pebbles or thorns.

Alexander felt bigger and bolder when mounted on horseback, as if he had discarded that side of his nature whose occasional timidity and cowardice so shamed and angered him. He had never had any formal riding lessons. Instead, he had picked up tips and guidance during rides with his grandmother and his aunt. He had been only five years old the first time he had gone for a ride on horseback (a short ride, with his grandmother leading the horse), at his grandparents' home at Limuru, in Kenya. He had also gone riding two or three times at his Aunt Mary's farm in the White Highlands. His love of riding was unlikely to be something he had inherited from his paternal line, for the Macleans on his father's side of the family had produced farmers and engineers. But at his grandmother Jeanie's childhood home in Mull, there had been horses, and horses also featured in her life on the large farm her father had bought when her family left the Isle of Mull for Kenya.

Alexander would sometimes ride out with Aunty Margaret, and occasionally with Granny Jeanie also, on a borrowed mount. They rode across the extensive uncultivated wasteland, akin to a very rough moorland, in which *vleis*, swamps, sand dunes and low scrub abounded, which ran from the edge of Fish Hoek town all the way across the Peninsula to Noordhoek and Long Beach. It was a wild piece of country, with few clear tracks, in which, had it not been for Chapman's Peak dominating the horizon to the north, it would have been easy to become somewhat disoriented. Near the southern end of Long Beach there were quicksands to be avoided, but the very wildness of the country appealed immensely to Alexander. Unless you reached Long Beach after the tide had turned, and firm damp sand was revealed by the retreating tide, there were few opportunities to get up to a long gallop in safety, but Alexander, who weighed less than nothing, but clung on with his legs and ankles, was at ease cantering down the sandy tracks, the salt-laden air blowing in his hair, for he only rarely wore a riding hat.

Sometimes as they left the stables they rode down to the seashore, and Alexander followed Aunty Margaret along Long Beach, all the way to Kommetjie, and Alexander thought it was a grand thing, clip-clopping through the village, and tying the horses up at the garden gate, and spending half an hour back at his grandparents' home, drinking orange juice and eating shortbread, cake or biscuits, before riding out through the village and all the way back – a distance of about three and a half miles – to the stables at Noordhoek.

By late September, with the coming of spring, the weather had grown very much warmer, and the Maclean family, accompanied by Stewart Fleming, visited Groot Constantia, the world famous wine estate with its grand, historic Cape Dutch manor house. Mrs. Fleming had once referred to the two boys, Alexander and Stewart, as "David and Jonathan," for they were together so much, the skinny blonde headed boy, and the almost equally skinny dark headed boy. But the friendship was not exclusive. Stewart would often be out on his bicycle with other friends after school, and Roy regarded him as a friend also. However, there was indeed a special bond between Stewart and Alexander, a bond which had been conceived during Alexander's first day at school. The two boys were able to make each other laugh: Stewart with his gift for mimicry, and Alexander with his wry, often self deprecating sense of humour. Already, aged eleven, Alexander had begun to appreciate the absurdity of the human condition. But there was more to their relationship than this: since that first day at school, and Stewart's introduction of Alexander into his circle of friends, Stewart had appointed himself as Alexander's protector. And for Alexander, his friendship with Stewart was experienced as something which made him feel warm and secure and unafraid.

Alexander, with his love of architecture and of ancient buildings, almost certainly enjoyed the visit to Groot Constantia more than Roy or Stewart did, but the setting, with its long straight avenue leading towards the house, running between double rows of oak trees, was a lovely one, dominated by the gracious old manor house with its beautifully proportioned, symmetrical façade and tall windows, and fine Cape Dutch gables, and its row of ancillary buildings to one side, which included the *jonkershuis*. There were vineyards reaching far into the distance on either side of the avenue, and the mountains formed a backdrop, and the boys were able to run around outside without causing anyone any bother.

For Alexander, the interior of the old house was beautiful and fascinating. He admired the broad, gleaming, polished yellowwood planking of the floors, the dark, heavy beamed, high ceilings of stinkwood, and the vaulted cellars beneath the house. He was captivated by the displays of magnificent eighteenth century and early nineteenth century porcelain, glassware and silver, and by the fine pieces of furniture, whose surfaces glowed with centuries of polish and care. When he got home later that afternoon he sat at the small desk in his room and began to sketch a floor plan of the manor house, as best he could remember it, and to draw the main façade. These sketches were among Alexander's earliest attempts at architectural drawing, only his efforts at sketching the floor plans of Aunt Mary's big old house, Hohenstein, having predated them. (Schematically accurate floor plans of the latter were impossible to achieve: Hohenstein was simply too vast for Alexander to have fixed the location of every room, on every floor, in his mind's eye). In the years to come, Alexander's passion for architecture was to see his architectural drawings becoming more and more detailed and precise, and he was to produce scores upon scores of architectural plans through the course of his adolescence and young manhood.

However, of all the many architectural designs Alexander produced, only one was ever to be translated into reality, and that was a house he designed, in the Cape Dutch idiom, for his brother. But that is part of a later story.

In November, Alexander, Stewart, Roy and another boy were walking home after school, with Roy and his friend trailing behind the two older boys.

'My Dad says we might be moving to Durban,' Stewart said suddenly to Alexander.

Alexander felt his stomach hollow out, and his heart thump suddenly.

'But when?' he exclaimed.

'I don't think anytime soon. I don't want to leave Cape Town.'

'I don't want you to go either!'

Alexander's fears of losing his friend cast a pall over his days, and his spirits were so low, he could not find it in him to look forward to Christmas.

'You're very long faced these days, Sandy,' his mother commented one day. 'What's wrong?'

'Nothing Mum.'

'Something is bothering you, Sandy. I know you too well not to know that.'

'Mum, why do things have to keep changing?'

'Nothing stays the same for ever. But what is it in particular that you're worrying about?'

'Stewart told me his family might have to move to Durban. I don't want Stewart to go away!'

'If the Flemings do move to Durban, it'll probably be a while away yet.'

'So it's true! They might be going away!'

'I don't think there are any definite plans at the moment. You cannot be scared of what might happen in the future, Sandy. All sorts of things might happen. You just have to enjoy and treasure the present.'

But Alexander was not comforted. He went down to the bottom of the garden and climbed over the wire mesh fence, and went and sat on the banks of the river. He blubbered a little, then knuckled his eyes and climbed back over the fence and went across the road.

'Is Stewart in, Mrs. Fleming?' he asked, when she answered his knock at their door.

'Yes, Alexander. You can go through to his room if you wish.' Stewart's mother never called him "Sandy."

'Thanks Mrs. Fleming,' Alexander replied. He found Stewart busy with some homework.

'Do you want to go for a ride, Stewart?'

But the boys did not cycle at all far. They followed the dirt track at the end of Mallaig Road, down to the river where the stepping stones provided a crossing, and dropped their bikes on the thick grass which grew there, and sat down on the grass, side by side. A pied kingfisher sat on the branch of a Port Jackson willow nearby, then began to bob its head up and down. Alexander saw it take off suddenly and swoop, and dive into the river, surfacing in a flurry of water droplets which caught the sun like a shower of silver, a tiny fish of the variety Alexander called a minnow, in its bill. The bird tossed its head back, its bill pointing up at the sky, and swallowed the fish.

After a long silence Alexander turned to his friend. 'Do you ever feel sad?' he asked him.

Stewart looked at him, a half smile on his face. 'Sometimes. Not often.'

If the Flemings were to go away, Alexander did not think his friend would miss him as much as he would miss Stewart. Alexander knew that he did not make friends easily. He knew that without Stewart, he would have been very lonely at school. He was afraid for the future.

Stewart reached his arm across his friend's shoulders. 'You think too much, Sandy!'

Alexander wished it could stay like this forever, his friend, with his arm across his shoulders, alongside him.

Chapter Nine

During the school's Christmas concert, Alexander sang a solo piece, standing all alone on the school stage before a hall packed with school children, their parents and their families. He sang *The Little Drummer Boy*. His high, clear treble rang out, his phrasing near perfect, for he had been coached well by Miss Armstrong.

Alexander's mother, seated with her husband about fifteen rows back from the stage, had to dab at her eyes with a handkerchief, and his father had to blow his nose at the end of the touching song. The audience clapped loudly.

Alexander's spirits had lifted as Christmas had drawn nearer. On Christmas Day, a Sunday, he awoke very early, feeling the excited anticipation that was usual for a Christmas morning. There was a bulging stocking hanging at the end of his bed that had not been there when he had gone to sleep. He explored its contents. There was a little Matchbox die cast car, and a large extra-soft eraser, suitable for Alexander's drawing and sketching, and a pencil sharpener, and a dozen chocolate fifty cent coins wrapped in gold foil, and a chrome plated whistle with a little ball inside, which he blew immediately. It emitted a shrill piercing sound. There was a greengage, his favourite fruit, and a twist of wrapping paper tied up with a piece of coloured string, from which spilled a shining *ironie* (a large polished metal ball bearing, much prized at school in games of marbles) and two big glass marbles and six smaller glass marbles, and there was a beautifully smooth, polished oblong of tiger's eye stone, a tawny, glowing colour, thus its name.

Beneath the festive tree, in a sitting room hung with bright paper decorations, were parcels wrapped in Christmas wrapping paper, which had not been there the night before either, but Alexander knew to wait for his parents to get up before opening those with his name on. He blew his whistle again, and Roy appeared in his cotton pyjamas with short pants which matched those that Alexander was wearing, and Roy turned on the Christmas tree lights, and their mother and father appeared soon after, both in light cotton dressing gowns, his father's red hair tousled and sticking up at the sides.

One of Alexander's great aunts in London had sent him a *Rupert Bear* annual, which although he was a little old for, he knew he would still enjoy. Roy's present from his great aunt was a book of games and puzzles. From their parents, each brother had a Corgi Toys die cast motor car, beautifully detailed. Alexander's was a two-tone Bentley Corniche; Roy's was a Ford Zephyr, also two-tone. Both cars had moulded interiors, glass headlights, and swivelling front wheels, operated by pressing slightly on one side or the other of the car, so that it could change direction. Roy also received two small boxed sets of extra Meccano parts, to add to his collection of Meccano. Alexander received a box of Minibricks pieces, which included two prized bow window units. Roy was given a book on aeroplanes from his grandparents in Kenya, while Alexander received a book about castles from the same source. These two books were still in the original brown paper package their grandmother had wrapped them in, which had been tied with string, and which was complete with franked Kenyan stamps on the parcel. The boys carefully tore off and removed the piece of wrapping paper with the

Kenyan stamps from the package, which they would later float off in warm water and add to their stamp collections.

The boys' father received a flat box containing four very large white cotton cambric handkerchiefs with the letters AM embroidered on each in red in one corner, and their mother got a Kenwood Chef food mixer.

'I'll have to teach Dorcas how to use it,' she thought to herself. However, Alex Maclean also gave his wife a very pretty locket of silver, set with an amethyst.

'Here, let me put it on you, Darling,' said the boys' father, and he fastened the silver chain around his wife's neck. 'What do you think, boys?' he asked.

'It's awfully pretty,' Alexander replied. His mother smiled at him, then kissed her husband on the cheek.

And there was a large box labelled "For my Three Boys, from Mum," and when Alexander was deputized to remove the wrapping paper, they found it was a very large scale Airfix plastic model kit of a vintage double decker London bus, complete with little bottles of paint, and two tubes of plastic glue, a gift which thrilled both the brothers and their father equally. Both Alexander and Roy asked their father if he would build it: it presented too great a challenge for them.

'Okeydoke,' Mr. Maclean replied, 'but the two of you must help me with painting some of the parts.'

The project kept their father and his sons busy at one end of the dining table for the next four weeks for an hour or so each evening, after Mr. Maclean's return from the office, during which period he would supervise his sons as they painted various small parts while they were still attached to the frames, or "trees", as their father called them. The boys' mother often sat down with them, so that she could chat with her family.

That Christmas morning, two big bowls of cashew nuts, a rare treat, appeared on the coffee table in the sitting room, and before the family had left for Kommetjie, both boys had helped themselves generously to the delicious nuts. This Christmas, the family was gathering at Granny Jeanie's house for Christmas lunch. Both their aunts would be there, and their Uncle William, and their cousins. By eleven o' clock that morning, as the family was setting out for Kommetjie (Mrs. Maclean carrying a bag in which were small gifts for the cousins), the temperature was already in the upper seventies Fahrenheit. The south-easter blew. That iconic cloud effect of summer, the table cloth, sat on top of Table Mountain. Otherwise, the sky was cloudless, a brilliant blue.

Mary Scott gave her father a bottle of Laphroaig Single Malt in a gift canister, and her brother received a bottle of Drambuie liqueur from her, which he opened after the huge Christmas lunch, and Jeanie Maclean fetched her lead crystal liqueur glasses from the glass fronted display cabinet, and each adult in the company drank some of the delicious liqueur. Then the adults retired to cushioned cane chairs on the shaded *stoep*, drinking coffee, while the maid cleared the dining table and began the washing up in the kitchen. (She had been persuaded to work on Christmas Day by being offered double wages for doing so). It had grown very warm in the dining room, and the fresh air was welcome, for by now the temperature in the shade was in the mid eighties Fahrenheit.

'Let's go down to Long Beach,' suggested James.

'Alright,' Alexander replied. He saw that his mother had dozed off – at least, her eyes were closed, and her mouth was open, and she was not moving, so he called out to his father 'Dad! We're going to Long Beach.'

'You're not going in the water, are you?'

'No, Dad.'

'Take care.'

Alexander, James, Tom and Roy walked slowly down the street towards the beach, their lunches weighing on them somewhat. At Long Beach there was the usual mob of holiday surfers. The waves at Long Beach were probably the best surfing waves on the entire west coast of the Peninsula, and were good year round, born from storms far out in the South Atlantic, in the Roaring Forties, and Kommetjie drew surfers of all degrees of skill from up and down the Peninsula, and one or two from as far afield as the United States and Australia. The boys sat down and lay back against a sandy white dune on which masses of succulent *vygies* grew, and gazed at the ocean view and at the young surfers, some of whom had their boards stuck vertically in the sand. Alexander, who would be turning twelve in two months' time, found the sight of the young men's tanned and sculpted bodies both compelling and disturbing, in a way he did not understand.

The four boys, all of whom were wearing their grey school shorts, with white shirts and long socks and polished black shoes, had not yet removed their ties, which their mothers had made them wear during the Christmas lunch. James now removed his tie, and the other boys immediately did likewise, stuffing them in their shorts pockets, and unbuttoning the tops of their shirts. After a while they got up and walked away from the main huddle of surfers, until the beach was clear, and they removed their shoes and socks and paddled at the edge of the water. The tide was coming in. The water felt icy cold to Alexander.

James began to jog along the edge of the incoming tideline, and Roy took off after him, with Tom following. With some reluctance, for he had eaten a great deal at lunch, Alexander followed the other three boys, splashing through the water. James came to a halt, laughing, and Alexander slowed down. 'I ate too much!' he declared.

'Me too,' James replied. 'And anyway, it's too hot to run today.'

'Yeah, it is,' Roy said.

'Let's walk back,' Alexander suggested.

By tea time the boys were feeling a little more energetic, and Roy and Tom were chasing each other in the garden. Alexander and James were playing in the garden with the toys they had received from their grandparents. Alexander had been given a US Army tank with an electric motor, whose turret revolved and which climbed over impressive obstacles with its ribbed rubber tracks; James had a dump truck, which had an electric motor which powered the tipper. At half past four tea was served by the maid, along with mince pies and a Christmas cake with thick marzipan icing. Alexander was extremely partial to marzipan, and he had a large slice of cake. The cake, like the Christmas pudding at the end of the lunch, had been made using real brandy.

The Scotts, the Boyds and the Macleans all left at the same time, at about six o' clock. The Macleans had furthest to drive, and, as was their habit (because it was such a beautiful drive, not to mention quicker, with far less traffic than Main Road), they took Chapman's Peak Drive. The Scotts and the Boyds, on their way to Hohenstein, would do likewise. It was still daylight when the Macleans got home at twenty past seven. Both brothers fussed over Simba, who had a lot to say to them, in between purring with relief to see the family back home, and Mrs. Maclean said 'I don't think we need any supper. If anyone is still hungry, I'll make toasted cheese.'

Both boys agreed that some toasted cheese would be nice. So did their father. After eating his toasted cheese, which had some thinly sliced tomato segments on top of the cheese, Alexander, who suddenly felt very tired indeed, said he was going to read in bed for a while. It was n't yet his bedtime, but he kissed his parents goodnight, and he hugged Simba, kissing the top of the cat's furry head, and Roy said goodnight to him, and he went to the bathroom to brush his teeth and use the lavatory. Then he sat up in bed and began to read Robert Louis Stevenson's *Kidnapped*, which Aunty Mary had given him. It had been a happy day. And there was no school tomorrow! He was soon asleep, and an hour later his mother came to tuck him properly into bed. He barely woke up while she was doing so.

The next day, Boxing Day, Dorcas was still away, but the day after Boxing Day she was back at work at the Macleans. Alexander's father gave her a Christmas box of ten Rand in a sealed envelope. 'Thank you Master,' she said. 'Happy Christmas to you and *Merrem.*'

'You must wish Dorcas a happy Christmas, boys,' their mother told them. They went to find Dorcas, who was vacuuming the sitting room carpet.

'Happy Christmas Dorcas,' Alexander told her.

'Yes, happy Christmas Dorcas,' Roy wished her.

Dorcas smiled and kissed each of the brothers on the cheek. 'And to you too my boys.'

In the early evening Alexander overheard his mother talking to his father. 'Apparently the poor old lady had been dead for about five days,' he heard her say. 'Her cat was hungry and dehydrated. It's been taken to the SPCA.'

'Oh no,' Alexander's father responded. 'Had no one been around over Christmas?'

'No, they had n't. Any more than we had.'

'I never even knew her name,' Alexander's father confessed.

'I knew she was called Mrs. Irwin, and that she was a widow, but that's all I knew about her,' Alexander's mother said.

Alexander felt the dawning of horror. He felt faint at the thought of old Mrs. Irwin, to whom some of the boys he knew had been so cruel, and against whom (and this was even worse) he had harboured casually uncharitable thoughts, dying, forgotten, at Christmas time, and worse – of her cat hungry and desperately thirsty, and alone in the house with its dead mistress. He rushed to his room, and began to sob quietly, tears of guilt, remorse, pity and shock. His voice thick with tears, he said 'And we were so horrible to her!'

He knew that Jonathan Van der Walt and Robbie had continued to torment the old lady, and he knew he should have told his parents what had been going on, and the sense that he was complicit in her continued torment, having been present on that one occasion last year, had distressed him whenever he had thought about it. But how could he confess something like that to his parents?

Alexander saw the framed sampler which his mother had embroidered as a girl, which hung on the wall above the head of his bed.

> *Thank you for the world so sweet,*
> *Thank you for the food we eat,*
> *Thank you for the birds that sing,*
> *Thank you, God, for everything.*

Reading these gentle words gave renewed strength to his tears of pity and remorse, but Alexander wept almost soundlessly. He did not wish anyone to ask him why he was crying. He found himself directing a silent prayer to a God he had never before truly prayed to, please to welcome the old lady's soul in Heaven. Alexander had repeated the sweet words from the sampler (with its embroidered illustrations of flowers and deer, rabbits and squirrels, around the border), on his knees every night before he went to bed, for as long as he could remember, and as a member of the school choir he sang the Lord's Prayer during term time at school assembly each morning. And when occasionally his family attended services at Saint Paul's church on a Sunday morning, he repeated the prayers along with the rest of the congregation, but in an unconsidered fashion. Alexander had never consciously prayed before. That unvoiced plea before God was his first conscious prayer ever: it was born of guilt, pity, sorrow and remorse. As he grew older, these sentiments were to empower many of Alexander's prayers.

At supper time he only played with his food. 'What's the matter, Sandy?' asked his mother. 'You look pale. Are n't you feeling well?'

'I'm alright, Mum.'

Mrs. Maclean leant across the table and put the back of her hand to his forehead. 'You don't seem to have a temperature. Why are n't you eating?'

'I just don't feel hungry.'

'I hope you're not coming down with something.'

At bed time Alexander kissed his mother and father goodnight, and went quietly to his bedroom. After the two brothers had left the sitting room, Mrs. Maclean said to her husband 'I hope Sandy is alright. He's been awfully quiet tonight. He does n't look well.'

'We'll see how he is in the morning,' Mr. Maclean replied.

Alexander remained subdued and quiet during that week between Christmas and New Year. His spirits rose a little however when on the 2nd of January his parents told the boys they would go watch the Coon Carnival, a parade of colourfully dressed minstrels, all of whom were drawn from among the Cape Coloured community of Cape Town. The Macleans drove into the City that morning, parking the car at the railway station opposite Garlicks department store in Adderley Street. They could hear the distant music from the marching bands, but they had time to position themselves in Saint George's Street behind Garlicks before the parade went by. Each group of musicians, separated by some distance from the next, was dressed in matching outfits of bright colours on which a great deal of attention had been lavished, and each group was playing a different tune, among which were some old favourites of the Western Cape, such as *Daar Kom die Alabama*, *Jan Pierewiet*, *Bobbejaan Klim die Berg*, and *Sarie Marais*. Alexander knew the words to these tunes, having been taught them at school during singing lessons, but he felt too bashful to join in when some among the crowd lining the pavement began to sing the words to them.

Once the last of the groups was past, the Maclean family began to follow the retreating bands up Saint George's Street towards the Gardens, where the boys were treated to milkshakes and sticky buns while they sat outside, shaded by oak trees in full leaf. The Gardens, nestling beneath the great looming bulk of the Mountain, were sheltered from the south-easterly breeze, and it was very warm. Mr. Maclean wore grey flannels, carefully pressed by Dorcas, an open necked shirt, a light sports jacket, and brown, highly polished Oxford brogues. The boys' mother was wearing a butter-yellow cotton frock and a cream, short sleeved cotton blouse. She had open toed sandals on her feet. The brothers wore pale blue shorts, cream short sleeved cotton shirts, and shoes with grey school socks reaching just below their knees. Unlike their neighbour Stewart Fleming, they rarely wore sandals. After walking around the park, which was a mass of blooms and colour at this season (the roses were particularly splendid), the family made their way down Adderley Street, Cape Town's main shopping street, towards the railway station car park, window shopping along the way. Once home again, Mrs. Maclean served her family cold ham with potato salad for lunch.

Alexander, still rather subdued, nonetheless felt something of the excitement of commencing a new school year when, in early January of 1967, he and Stewart began standard five, their final year of primary school. They were now among the top dogs at school. During that first term however, Alexander quite often shunned company, preferring to be alone. The possibility that Stewart was likely to be leaving sometime soon preyed on his mind, but it was his brooding on Mrs. Irwin's lonely death over Christmas that caused him the greatest unhappiness. Worse even than the thought of a tormented old woman dying alone at Christmas, was the image of a distressed, hungry and thirsty cat.

'The cat could have died,' he thought.

Chapter Ten

Alexander was hurting. He longed to confess his own part, if only as a reluctant witness, in Mrs. Irwin's torment, but he was scared of the revulsion his parents would feel for him if he did so. The Macleans, for all their not very distant Catholic ancestry, were not of course Catholics anymore. But what Alexander needed, had he only known it, was a priest to talk to. However, he had only the vaguest idea of what Catholicism was, and no idea that the sacrament of confession existed in the Catholic Church.

There were moments when the old Alexander reappeared for a short while. He was more like himself on his twelfth birthday, which fell that year on a Sunday. Alexander received a wonderfully illustrated book on ocean liners from his parents, which delighted him. He looked forward to getting stuck into it later that day.

'The *Europa* is there – we checked,' his father said. The *MS Europa* was the Lloyd Triestino liner aboard which the Macleans had made their Mombasa – Cape Town voyage, a voyage which had been one of the highlights of Alexander's life to date (along with the voyage in a British India liner from Mombasa to London Docks when he was five or six years old, and the family's subsequent return to Kenya in a Bristol Britannia four engined turboprop airliner). Alexander also received a Matchbox *Models of Yesteryear* vintage Rolls Royce Silver Ghost car, a gleaming silver in colour. His grandmother in Kenya had sent him a Kenyan first day postal cover for his stamp collection.

The Scotts – his Aunt Mary and his cousins, James and Tom – and the Boyds – his Aunt Margaret, with Uncle William and their two little girls – had come down from the mountainside to visit that day, and Aunty Mary gave Alexander a *Tintin* book for his birthday. His Aunt Margaret gave him a beautifully illustrated nineteenth century children's classic, *At the Back of the North Wind*, by George MacDonald, the author of *The Princess and the Goblin*, and *The Princess and Curdie* (two stories which Alexander enjoyed reading over and over). Alexander felt he had done well this birthday – and he was yet to receive his gift from Granny Jeanie and Grandpa Rory.

The three families set off together. The Scotts joined the Macleans in the Vauxhall, with the three adults sitting on the bench seat in front, and the four boys on the rear seat. The Boyds following in their Holden station wagon. They took Main Road and drove past Muizenberg, and on towards Kalk Bay, with its fishing harbour. The weather – very warm, with a burning sun in a clear blue sky – was typical for late February in Cape Town. The other boys' high spirits raised Alexander's own spirits, and he was soon bickering and laughing along with them. Aunt Mary had proposed the outing. They were to take a boat trip to Seal Island, lying far out in False Bay. Alexander, with his passion for boats, felt tremendously excited.

Harbours and boats fascinated Alexander. Kalk Bay harbour was home to a sizable fishing fleet, and a number of the sturdy, beamy, high prowed wooden fishing boats were tied up alongside the quays. As Alexander walked past them with his family and relations, he could smell the aromas the boats gave off: sun-warmed wood, paint, fish, and diesel oil. There were some Coloured crew (their skin burned the colour of mahogany by the sun, some of them stripped to the waist, their corded muscles sharply defined in the bright sunlight) who were doing maintenance work on these boats, yelling good naturedly to one another.

Against the farthest quay a big cabin cruiser, the *Carlota*, was tied up. The party made their way to it, and Mr. Maclean shouted 'Ahoy the *Carlota!*' as they approached the vessel. A swarthy white man in his late thirties or early forties, with a Portuguese look to him, who had not shaved for a day or two, and was wearing a rather worn and not very clean blue jacket with brass buttons, a battered captain's cap, and off-white trousers whose turn-ups gathered in folds at his OK Bazaars *takkies*, appeared from within the boat, and Mr. Maclean asked him 'Are you headed for Seal Island soon?'

'*Ja*, I'll take you there Sir. It's five Rand for adults and three Rand for children.'

Alexander's father began to take out his wallet, but his sister Mary said 'No, Alex. This was my idea. It's my treat for the birthday boy.'

'Well ... that's very kind of you, Mary. Are you sure?'

'Of course. Let's see ... how much does that come to?'

'Forty-three Rand.'

Mary Scott counted out forty-five Rand, and gave the wad of notes to her brother, who smiled and said 'Thanks Sis,' then passed them to the boat's unprepossessing captain, who began laboriously to count them. 'Sandy, you take my hand,' Mr. Maclean continued. 'Roy – you take Mummy's hand.' The adults, each of whom was leading or carrying at least one child, mounted the short gangway and stepped aboard the boat.

'I hope I'm not going to be seasick,' Mrs. Maclean said to her husband.

'I don't think you will, Livia. I'd say it's only the slow movements of the big ships that do that to you.'

Alexander's mother looked doubtful.

A Coloured crewman appeared from below, and the boat's captain disappeared into the wheelhouse, and shortly thereafter the engines fired up with a deep rumble. Alexander felt almost unbearably excited. The Coloured crewman hauled in the short gangway and lashed it horizontally to the boat's railings, and yelled in Afrikaans at some of the crew on the nearest fishing boat, who came and slipped the mooring ropes forward and aft from the bollards to which they had been attached, and the *Carlota's* crewman hauled them aboard. The big boat's engines increased their rumbling, and the boat drew away from the quayside. One of the Coloured fishermen waved at the boat, and Alexander and James, who were leaning up against the railing, waved back. The engines' rumbling increased in pitch yet again, and the vessel picked up speed and left the harbour.

Immediately they began to feel the boat pitch and roll, as the south-easter, which was blowing strongly, took it abeam. With one accord, all four boys went forward to the bows, and yelled with excitement as the engines increased their revolutions once again and the boat surged forward. It took only one partial drenching from a sheet of spray for the four boys to retreat from the bows and stand amidships in a row together at the portside, or lee railing. The women and the little girls had already taken shelter down below in the saloon, leaving only Alexander's father and Uncle William to watch over the four boys. But the wind was cold across the water, and the boys were not entirely dry, and before long they too descended the steep stairs and took shelter in the saloon, which was a large cabin amidships, with a rather Spartan interior and hard seats. Alexander, however, was happy, too happy and excited to feel cold. He stared out the oblong window alongside his seat, watching the shore receding rapidly, the buildings growing smaller and smaller.

'Are you feeling alright, Livia?' Mr. Maclean asked his wife after a while. Alexander's mother did not look very well. Her face had acquired a shiny, greenish pallor.

'No. I'm not.' Mrs. Maclean stood up suddenly and said 'Going to be sick.'

Mr. Maclean took his wife's arm and they left the saloon. He returned alone after about five minutes.

'Will Olivia be alright?' Mary Scott asked her brother.

'I left her at the stern. She's been sick over the side of the boat. I should n't have made her join us. It was stupid of me. Olivia has never been a good sailor.'

Alexander however could spare little thought for his mother's sufferings. 'Let's go back outside,' he said.

'Alright,' James responded. 'You guys coming with us?' he asked Roy and Tom.

So all four boys made their way back up the steep, narrow staircase and stepped out onto the deck, and Mr. Maclean followed them, to keep an eye on them. No one was wearing life jackets. Alexander had never felt the least twinges of seasickness on the voyages he had made so far on ocean liners; nor had Roy. Their father also was a stranger to seasickness. So too it appeared were James and Tom. Indeed, Alexander took a positive delight in the boat's pitching and rolling. He gazed at the sea, a deep cobalt blue on whose undulating surface the strong wind had thrown up fairly steep little waves crested with white horses, all moving in a north-westerly direction. The occasional burst of spray flew back from the bows and made the boys step back hastily from the railing. They laughed with delight each time this happened. The boys and Mr. Maclean were all standing against the port railings, the bulk of the wheelhouse sheltering them from the south-easter.

At Seal Island, an expanse of rock-hewn outcrop rising shallowly from the sea, the children wrinkled their noses at the powerful aroma from the seal colony, as the *Carlota* circled the island slowly at a distance. The water had seals sporting in it, and some of these animals, with their appealing, bewhiskered, snub snouts, stuck their sleek heads out of the water to gaze at the boat. Mrs. Maclean was sick once again over the stern.

Once the boat had set her return course, the boys went below again. No one was dressed for the wind, which was so much colder over the water than it had been on land, and the saloon seemed rather attractive now. Alexander's father however went to join his suffering wife at the boat's stern.

Mrs. Maclean, her legs unsteady, and looking terrible, needed a hand down the short gangway at the quayside. The boys all ran down the gangway before any of the adults could think to grab their hands. Only Margaret Boyd's little girls were taken in charge; Jenny, the oldest, held her mother's hand, while Mary, the youngest, was carried by Uncle William. Once on the solid and immovable quayside, Alexander's mother expressed a heartfelt 'Never again.' Her husband held her by the arm as the group made their way back to the two cars, Mr. Maclean apologising to his wife for having taken her on the boat trip.

It was by now nearing lunch time, and the party drove on to Fish Hoek, and out along the Kommetjie Road, and so to Jeanie and Rory Maclean's home, where they were to have lunch and spend the afternoon. Alexander was thrilled with his present from his grandparents, a Buntline Special six-shooter cap gun, but during lunch, his mother sat nibbling at a piece of bread, spurning the roast chicken and delicious golden baked potatoes which Granny Jeanie served. But Mrs Maclean's face had regained a little colour, and having washed it in the bathroom, it no longer had an unhealthy sheen to it.

Later that afternoon, Alexander's father approached his sister quietly and pressed twenty Rand upon her. 'Forty-three Rand is quite a whack,' he said to her. 'Here, take this. I wont have any argument.' Mary Scott, having accepted the notes, leaned forward and kissed her brother on the cheek.

In early June the weather turned much cooler, and damp, as the first winter rains arrived. Alexander suffered such a severe asthma attack while at weekly soccer practice at school one afternoon that an ambulance was called. For Alexander, it was a terrifying experience. He had feared he was asphyxiating. As he lay recovering at Cape Town's Groote Schuur Hospital, the recollection of the experience was to go some way towards reshaping his outlook on life. Horror, he now knew, did happen. The extremes of suffering and terror existed, and they would not always pass him by. And he could no longer take for granted that his parents would always be able to spare him the worst of life's horrors. They had not spared him this. This dark, near despairing attitude remained with Alexander for several days after he was discharged from hospital the day following the asthma attack. He took away something else also: that this terrifying experience had been a punishment both for his part in the torment of old Mrs. Irwin, and for his uncharitable thoughts whenever he had happened to see her as he walked home from school.

Alexander did not think in terms of "sin". His family were not frequent enough churchgoers, and he had not been exposed often enough to the theological concept of sin, to have internalised such a cosmic proposition, but he believed instinctively in its existence, even if "sin" was not then what he called it. Alexander was to be aware of the existence of sin, and of the danger, via its indulgence, of giving oneself over to punishment, for the rest of his days.

Already cast down by these dark thoughts, Alexander listened as his friend Stewart told him, in late June, that his family was moving to Durban the following month, during the school holidays. Despite his growing inclination to solitude, Alexander had sustained his friendship with Stewart, although he joined Stewart's group at school less often than he had the year before, spending time – if at all – with Stewart after school in the afternoons. At those times when Alexander was not alone, he was to be found either with his brother, Roy, or with Stewart Fleming. He pursued no other friendships. His friendship with Stewart represented the sum total of his social life.

'My Dad says I can begin the new school in Durban with the start of third term,' Stewart told Alexander.

Alexander had known for some time that he was going to have to say goodbye to Stewart sooner rather than later. But hearing it told to him as an imminent certainty made him feel scared. He met his friend's green eyed gaze, and observed with a fresh clarity of perception Stewart's rather fine features and narrow face, which still carried something of the summer's tan.

'I wish you were n't going away!' Alexander declared in an anguished tone. He was afraid that it would break his heart when Stewart left for Durban. It would have been easier if Alexander had had other friends, but he did not: the other boys he knew from school were well disposed acquaintances, at best.

'Me too. I like it here. I wont know anyone there.'

By the coming Saturday the cold front, with its damp weather, had lifted, and the day dawned fair; windless, dry and sunny. Alexander accompanied his family to Rondebosch town centre later that morning, taking with him some of the pocket money he had saved up. The air, washed clean by the rain, had a wonderful clarity to it; glowing and luminous. Alexander visited the CNA, the stationers and booksellers, and after examining what they had on their shelves, he bought an address book bound in faux black leather. Back home, Alexander wrote his name and address inside it. But he had been made thoughtful beyond his years, and he had no faith in his family remaining for any length of time at Mallaig Road, so he also wrote down his grandparents' names and their Kommetjie address. Then, using his Pelikan fountain pen, he wrote on the inside cover, in his flowing italic script "For my friend Stewart, whom I will always remember. Sandy."

Alexander showed the gift to his mother. 'What a lovely idea,

Sandy! It's very thoughtful of you. I am sure Stewart will be very pleased with it.'

'You see, Mum – I've written Granny Jeanie's and Grandpa Rory's address also, in case we move soon.'

Mrs. Maclean felt a pang, at the sudden realisation of her first born's loss of certainty in his life. Both she and her husband had always assumed, without thinking about it much, that children were infinitely flexible and adaptable. For the first time, she understood that perhaps this was not so. At least, not for Sandy. On a sudden whim she did something she very rarely did: she hugged her son, and kissed him on the forehead. He was not much shorter than she was now.

'Whatever happens,' she said, 'we'll always be together.'

On a damp mid winter's late afternoon, beneath a lowering, grey sky (it had rained much of that day, and would rain again), Alexander sat in Stewart's bedroom, which looked strangely gutted of Stewart's personality, for his personal possessions had been packed up, ready for the removals van which was arriving the following morning. Feeling self conscious, Alexander gave Stewart the address book he had bought him.

'It's very nice,' Stewart said. 'Thanks, Sandy.'

'You see, I've written my grandparents' address also, in case we move away. Then you'll still be able to write to me.'

'Good thinking,' Stewart said. 'I'll ask Mum for our new address, so you can write to me.'

'Yeah, I'ld like that.'

The boys found a harassed Mrs. Fleming in the kitchen, feeding Annie, Stewart's little sister, some chocolate, because she had been blubbering. Alexander was grateful he did not have a baby sister. 'Mum,' Stewart said, 'where's our Durban address? I want to give it to Sandy.'

'Oh – it's on the quote from the removals company. In the top drawer.'

Stewart found the document in the kitchen drawer. 'Where can I write this down, Mum?'

'There should be a notebook and a pen there. Tear a page from the notebook, Stewie.'

With the Flemings' Durban address on a piece of paper in his pocket, Alexander walked with Stewart down to the end of Mallaig Road, where they could watch the river, which was in flood. It felt cold. It began to rain again.

'Let's go to my place,' Alexander said.

The two friends made their way to Alexander's bedroom, where Stewart sat on the chair at the desk, and Alexander sat on the bed. They talked for a while, but the conversation was stilted. After a while Stewart said 'I'ld better be getting back.'

'Well … I suppose this is goodbye.'

'Yeah. There wont be time to say goodbye tomorrow morning.'

'Goodbye then, Stewart. I hope it all works out for you in Durban. It'll be a lot warmer there!'

Stewart laughed. 'Yeah, maybe it wont be too bad. We'll write, Sandy.'

'Yes, we will.'

The boys made their way slowly to the Macleans' front door, where Stewart thrust out his hand, and Alexander took it and shook it. He could not remember the last time he had shaken hands with anyone – oh, it would have been with the minister the last time they had gone to church. He felt a suspicious trembling of the lower lip.

'Good luck,' he said.

'You too. Thanks for the address book.' And Stewart turned and ran across the road through renewed rain, and Alexander was never to talk with him again.

Alexander suspected that he did not deserve to know happiness. Stewart's departure was part of the punishment he felt was due him. Alexander wished however that he could have told Stewart how much his friendship had meant to him, how much he was going to miss him, but how could he have said these things? They did write, however. They exchanged a couple of letters each during the remainder of 1967, and one each during the first quarter of 1968, by which time the Macleans had indeed left Mallaig Road, and were living in Johannesburg. But thereafter their correspondence dried up, and although Alexander was often to think of Stewart Fleming, he was never to know what sort of a man Stewart had grown up to be, or how he earned a living, or whether he had a family of his own. Parting from Stewart was Alexander's first heartache, but there would be many more heartaches to come, and some of them very soon.

Alexander's maternal grandfather had been born in Portsmouth, to a Royal Navy family. He was educated at Christ's Hospital, known as the Bluecoat School, in the City of London. The boys' distinctive yellow stockings encouraged the London urchins to yell "Baby's yaller!" at them, or so Alexander's grandfather wrote in his memoirs. He had joined the Royal Navy at the age of sixteen, and was duly commissioned. He was the third generation of Copelands to hold a commission in the Royal Navy. He had met and married Alexander's grandmother in London shortly after the Great War, and not long thereafter the two newlyweds had emigrated to the young colony of Kenya. When he retired he had been the head of the Kenya Coastal Tourism Association. He and Alexander's grandmother lived in Mombasa, and Alexander had not seen them since the family's departure from Kenya in early 1965. In August 1967 the old man died.

Alexander had not known his maternal grandfather as well as he knew Grandpa Rory, for Alexander and his family had lived in Nairobi, several hundred miles inland from Mombasa. But his family had stayed with his grandparents for almost two weeks prior to the Macleans' departure from Mombasa for South Africa, at their very pretty villa overlooking Mombasa harbour, in whose garden spectacular flamboyants, or flame trees grew, and whose veranda was covered in pink Bougainvillea. During that time Alexander had grown close to his mother's father, with whom he found he shared an interest in history, and a love of the sea and ships. Grandpa Harry Copeland was a gentle, courtly old man, invariably dressed in a tropical white linen suit, and sitting at his desk, hand rolling his cigarettes, he had talked to Alexander not as if he were a child, but as if he were another adult. Alexander felt sadness, a sense of loss, when his grandfather died, but he was uncertain what his mother was feeling. Mrs. Maclean did not tend to exhibit her emotions. In fact, she was deeply distressed at her father's death, and she wished to visit her mother in Kenya.

The boys and their father drove Mrs. Maclean to Cape Town's D. F. Malan Airport, where she would catch a flight for Johannesburg, and at Jan Smuts Airport she would catch another flight for Nairobi, and then a third flight for Mombasa. The boys' mother was away for two weeks. Fortunately they had Dorcas to attend to their domestic needs for five and a half days a week during the next two weeks, or the house's domestic economy would have fallen apart, for Mr. Maclean, brought up in Kenya with a host of servants, could not even boil an egg. He learned very quickly however, not only how to boil an egg, but how to fry them, during the two weeks that his wife was away. In this exercise both boys participated.

'Dad, can you cook mince?' Alexander asked his father the first Sunday evening of his mother's absence.

'Let's see what we've got in the fridge,' Alexander's father replied. The boys and their father went to examine the fridge's contents. They found a block of minced beef, but it was in the small freezer compartment at the top of the fridge, and it was frozen solid.

'Do you think we can defrost this in time for supper?' Mr. Maclean asked his sons.

'I don't think so, Dad,' Alexander replied. 'It takes quite a few hours to thaw food.'

'Well, what can we do for now?'

'Dad, how about toasted cheese? With sliced tomatoes?'

'That sounds good.'

Mr. Maclean removed a large block of cheddar and began to slice it into thin slices. 'With Mum away I see how ignorant I am. You boys know much more about cooking than I do.'

'We've watched Mum and Dorcas sometimes, that's all,' Alexander replied.

Fortunately for the Maclean menfolk, Dorcas prepared a supper for them each weekday before she left for her own home, and all it needed was reheating that evening. In this exercise the brothers directed their father. But Dorcas was not there to cook their breakfasts before the boys left for school, and their father left for work. Nor was she there on Sunday. However, the boys and their father survived, thanks to cold meats and boiled and fried eggs and toasted cheese and grilled fish fingers, and they were not noticeably thinner when they drove to the airport to collect Mrs. Maclean.

Alexander's mother had small gifts, keepsakes and curios from Kenya, for her sons. Alexander had missed his mother very much indeed, and he felt a spilling over of joy and relief to have her back. He had thought of her every day while she had been away, and he had felt her absence particularly in the evenings. He had also been remembering his grandfather, and he felt it was a great pity that he had hardly known him before the final two weeks the family had spent with his grandparents at the coast. On previous visits to the coast, he had been too young to fully appreciate his grandfather. Harry Copeland had led such an interesting, at times exciting, life, and now Alexander would never talk to him again. It was during one such moment of personal grief that Alexander came to spare a thought for how his mother and grandmother might be feeling, and, his own emotions ever close to the surface, he had wept a little as he did so.

And Alexander feared that perhaps Grandpa Harry's death had been a punishment for the part he had played – however reluctantly – in old Mrs. Irwin's torment, and for his unkind thoughts towards her. Alexander struggled to despatch these irrational fears, but he did not succeed.

'But Grandpa Harry was old, seventy-eight years old!' he thought to himself.

'What did Grandpa die of?' Alexander asked his mother.

'A heart attack, Sandy,' his mother replied.

Alexander looked at his mother, and he thought she looked sad. He wished to tell her he felt sad too. But how could he, when perhaps Grandpa's death was a punishment for his own wickedness?

With the coming of summer, Alexander cycled for the first time, in company with his brother, to Rondebosch Public Library. Up until now, the brothers had relied on their mother to take them to the library by car. Alexander was to cycle to the library often that summer, occasionally accompanied by Roy on his bicycle, but more often alone. Alexander preferred to be alone on these rides. He could think about Stewart, and remember his grandfather, without others disturbing his thoughts – as invariably happened at home. The public library was located in a building Alexander enjoyed visiting, for it was a rather grand Victorian edifice, with a magnificent double staircase leading to the children's library on the first floor. This was quite a bike ride for him, as Rondebosch town centre was some distance from the Maclean house on Mallaig Road. These early indications of a venturesome and independent streak in Alexander's character were to become pronounced once he had attained adulthood.

Chapter Eleven

Shortly before he died, Harry Copeland had published his memoirs in Kenya. Born in 1889, the Royal Navy he joined still belonged to the ironclads era, with battleships possessing only four big guns in two turrets, and a plethora of smaller guns. But by the time he was commissioned, the *Dreadnought* had entered service, and she revolutionised naval warfare. This battleship carried ten twelve inch guns in five turrets, and no intermediate guns. (She was however armed with twenty-seven quick-firing three inch guns for defence against torpedo boats).

And, with partially oil fired steam turbine engines, she was faster than any existing battleship, having a genuine top speed of twenty-one knots, instead of the optimistic but generally unattainable standard of eighteen knots that had thus far prevailed, and she had far more reliable engines with which to deliver a top speed over longer periods of time.

For several decades, all battleships were thereafter referred to as "dreadnoughts". Their gunnery officers pursued an increasingly technical path, and it was gunnery which Alexander's grandfather chose to specialise in. He was present at the Battle of Jutland, which the Imperial German Navy won on points, but which the Royal

Navy won in terms of strategy: after the battle the field was theirs, and never again could the German navy pose a serious threat to the Royal Navy. The naval armaments race, which was a major factor leading to war in 1914, ended at Jutland. And with its ending, and a lengthy period of naval contraction looming, Alexander's grandfather felt that opportunities for further promotion would be scarce, and far apart. He resigned his commission, and in London in 1924 he met and married a young American girl born and raised in France, and they moved to Kenya, which was still a young colony, as yet barely settled by Europeans.

There, he worked at a variety of jobs, but he became well known and respected in time along the Kenya coast, first as an hotelier, and later, as the head of the Kenya Coastal Tourism Association. His memoirs made fascinating reading, and they represented the first time that Alexander had read, from cover to cover, a lengthy work of non-fiction written for adults. Alexander was immensely proud of his mother's father, and proud also of the fact that King William IV, Queen Victoria's uncle, had been his grandfather's great-great-grandfather, and that he, Alexander, therefore shared an ancestral bloodline in part with the British royal family.

But now his grandfather was gone, and he would never again be able to talk to him about the sea and ships, and about the fabulous islands of the Indian Ocean, and the Arab seamen who had navigated those waters, waters with which Sinbad had been familiar. Nor would he be able again to listen to his grandfather tell tales from his time in the Royal Navy, a career which had spanned both the Mediterranean and the North Atlantic, and which had seen him decorated by Abdul Hamid II, the Sultan of Turkey (who was to become known in Europe as Abdul the Damned, or the Bloody Sultan, for the slaughter of between one hundred thousand to three hundred thousand Armenians within the Turkish empire during his reign). Alexander had never before been as conscious of his links with the past as he had become during the almost two weeks his family had stayed with his grandparents in Mombasa. Now that old man, such a beloved living link with the past, was gone. Alexander grieved for his loss.

And he grieved for the loss of his friend, Stewart.

But there were some happy times still to come through the remainder of that year. At such times Alexander was able to escape the brooding, solitary mood which seemed to possess him so much of the time. There were the weekend visits to Alexander's grandparents in Kommetjie to look forward to, where Granny Jeanie lavished affection and hugs and shortbread and cakes upon her grandchildren. Alexander went riding sometimes with Aunt Margaret, and his family visited his aunts and his cousins at Hohenstein, that magical house on the side of the mountain, with many of its topmost rooms all closed up and left to moulder in peace, undisturbed by any but the owls that could sometimes be heard hooting in the early hours high up in the upper floors of the house as they returned from a night's hunting. Hohenstein was a child's fairytale playground, so vast that even during the winter, when the rain was teeming down outside, or the cold mist was swirling around the house, there was ample space indoors to conduct energetic physical pursuits and games with cousins James and Tom. In the summertime there were the large grounds in which to play and have adventures, with their woods and the mountain fed stream, and the vineyard where in late summer the Coloured pickers would harvest the grapes, which were loaded onto the backs of open lorries and taken to be trodden and to become in due course a superior wine, which was retailed in bottles with a label featuring a sepia tinted photograph of Hohenstein.

During his third term in standard five, in very early spring, Alexander's class was taken on an excursion to the Cape Town Castle, and for Alexander, with his love of old buildings and his interest in history, this was a fascinating visit. The Castle of Good Hope is a five bastion star shaped fort built in the seventeenth century by the Dutch East India Company. The smooth faced walls built of stone slope slightly inwards, and each bastion commands a wide angle of fire for the canon that were originally mounted atop them. For South Africans (and for people like Alexander, who admired ancient structures) the Castle was deeply significant, being the oldest surviving building in South Africa, its pentagonal star shape adopted by the South African Defence Force as an emblem.

'When the Castle was built by the Dutch East India Company,' their History teacher told them, as the children gathered before the main gateway, which was surmounted by an elegant bell tower, 'it was situated on the coastline of Table Bay, and was partially surrounded by a moat fed by the Salt River, and it could protect the settlement from sea-born attack, and protect the burgers from an attack by land also.'

'Sir, why is the Castle so far back from the sea now?' asked one of the brighter boys.

'Good question, Vincent. Over time, much land was reclaimed from the sea, thus pushing the coastline further and further away from the Castle,' their teacher replied.

The children jostled their way through the tunnelled entranceway, and saw ahead of them a wide, deep court as big as a parade ground, across the width of which ran a three story building painted in yellow ochre, like all the interior buildings in the Castle. In the centre of this building was a balcony, which was, the children's teacher told them, 'De Kat balcony, and here important announcements were made to the Cape Town burgers. If you turn around and look up at the pediment above the gateway, you can see an extremely beautiful example of work by the late eighteenth century architectural sculptor, Anton Anreith.'

Alexander gazed all around him, very susceptible to the atmosphere of age and history which surrounded him. This colonial child born and raised in Africa, who was barely five or six years old the last time his family had travelled to Britain, could only once before remember ever having seen any building quite so ancient and, in sheer size and range, quite so impressive: that had been Fort Jesus, the truly ancient fortress built by the Portuguese at Mombasa. But Cape Town Castle was surely the oldest structure he had seen since leaving Kenya. Most of the boys with him were similarly impressed, if less consciously interested in the architecture, for Cape Town Castle occupied an important place in the national iconography of South Africa, and was, after all, a military structure.

For Alexander, the William Fehr collection of paintings and antique furniture housed within this central range of buildings was almost overwhelmingly beautiful. The contents of the Castle Military Museum were of interest to most of the boys. One of the highlights of the tour saw the children herded into one of the ancient cells deep within the immensely thick walls, where luckless prisoners in the past had been kept in stygian darkness. Pressed uncomfortable close together, the sense of constraint and weighty stone bearing in upon them, there were shrieks from the girls and yells from some of the boys also, when the door to the cell was slammed shut by the Castle guide and the light was turned off. Alexander felt his throat constrict, and panic began to flutter close by him, and he experienced enormous relief when, amidst uncertain laughter, the light was once again turned on, and the cell door was opened. He jostled with the other children in the doorway, keen to get outside as quickly as possible.

Alexander was to fear and shun dark, constricted spaces the rest of his life, and he was to remember how he had felt, momentarily trapped in that awful cell in the Castle walls, even in his late middle age. But for the next several weeks, sitting at his desk in his bedroom, Alexander, inspired by this visit, was to draw and sketch plans of quadragonal bastion forts protected by moats and looking out across the sea, creations of his own enormously fertile imagination. (He tried repeatedly to work out ways of getting the five sides of equal length, and the angles equal also, in pentagonal designs, but in this he could not succeed. It required a command of geometry way beyond the level he had thus far attained).

When the Macleans had first moved into their house in Mallaig Road, the plot directly opposite them was standing empty. In 1966 however, a house was built on it, and its roof obscured the clear view of the Mountain that the Macleans had previously enjoyed. The family who moved into the house were pleasant, quiet people, with just one child, a boy in his mid teens named Michael who went to Rondebosch Boys' High. The Maclean brothers were to come to know and like him over time. He had a quiet, self confident manner. Michael was always kind and patient with the two boys, and they enjoyed admiring his collection of Airfix and Revell plastic kit models. Michael shared Alexander's interest in ships. It was clear to Alexander that Michael knew a good deal about ships, and several of the kits that Michael had built were ship models. Alexander yearned especially to possess the wonderfully detailed scale model of the Mississippi River paddle boat, the Robert E. Lee, which Michael had built.

'The Mississippi River paddle boats carried passengers in great luxury, Sandy,' Michael told him. 'You must imagine beautifully decorated public saloons with high ceilings, and carved woodwork, and some of the cabins had real brass bedsteads in them, and the side decks would have been piled high with bales of cotton.'

Alexander was carried away by his imagination. He remembered seeing a western once with his family, at either the Sunset or Goodwood drive-in cinema, which featured a Mississippi River paddle boat, with card sharps and gamblers in fancy waistcoats drinking whiskey late into the night in the saloon, and beautiful ladies with big bosoms in lovely outfits leaning over their shoulders. How he wished to possess that model of the Robert E. Lee!

In the early summer of 1967, Michael told the Maclean brothers that he was getting rid of many of his plastic kit models, and would they like any of them?

'Oh yes please!' both the brothers declared.

'Come and choose the ones you want, then,' Michael said.

Roy chose mostly fighter planes, while Alexander chose five model ships, including the much desired Robert E. Lee.

'Oh, my boys … where will you keep them?' their mother asked despairingly.

'Mum, we'll make room,' they replied. Roy told her he would suspend the airplanes from the ceiling.

'If Dad says that's alright,' Mrs. Maclean told her youngest son. The next weekend, Mr. Maclean and Roy hung the half dozen or so model airplanes from the ceiling in his bedroom. Alexander had lined up three of the model ships atop his bookcase, and the remaining two on his bedroom windowsill. He could gaze at these models over and over, in particular, at the Mississippi River paddle boat. They inspired a search by Alexander at the public library in Rondebosch for books in which these ships featured, and they gave rise to a collection of drawings Alexander worked on for several weeks, of highly imaginative cross sections of the various ships. One Sunday morning, not long after Michael had gifted the brothers with these models, Alexander saw Michael and his family returning from church. He ran across the street with Roy a little while later and rang their front door bell. Michael's father, a rather stern faced gentleman with a moustache, came to the door.

'Good morning sir,' Alexander greeted him. 'Can Michael come to our house? I want to show him what we've done with the models he gave us.'

'Alright Alexander, I'll call him.'

Michael was still dressed in his churchgoing grey school slacks and a white long sleeved shirt, but he had removed his tie. He smiled at the brothers. 'How are you guys?'

'We're fine,' they replied. 'Come and see how nice your models look, Michael!'

The older boy followed them across the street. He admired the way Roy had suspended the fighter planes from the ceiling, and he said to Alexander 'I think you're as keen on ships as I am, Sandy.'

'Yeah … I'm very interested in ships. Did you know we've been on three ocean liners already, Michael?' ("Ocean liner" was a term Alexander had learned when his parents had given him a book on passenger ships for his birthday. He enjoyed the sound of it, and he was pleased of the opportunity of using it now).

'Really? Where did you go?' Michael responded.

'We went to England twice,' Roy told him.

'And when we left Kenya we came to South Africa by sea,' Alexander said.

'You're lucky blokes,' Michael responded. 'I've never made a sea voyage.'

Mrs. Maclean asked Michael whether he would like some chocolate chip biscuits. 'And some tea?'

'Yes, please, Mrs. Maclean. That would be nice.'

So the brothers sat at the table in the kitchen with their friend from across the road and all three munched on chocolate chip biscuits, and while Michael had a cup of tea, the two brothers drank orange juice. Alexander gazed at Michael from beneath his lashes. The older boy had fresh faced, open features and curly light brown hair. Alexander was inclined to hero worship Michael.

'I'm going to Rondebosch Boys' High next year,' Alexander told the older boy.

'You'll like it there. It's a great school. I expect we'll see each other from time to time.'

'I 'ld like that,' Alexander responded.

Michael thanked Mrs. Maclean for the biscuits and the tea, and said he must be getting home now.

'I'll be seeing you guys,' Michael said.

'Yeah, thanks for the model ships and the planes.'

Michael grinned. 'You did me a favour. My Mum was getting a little tired of all my models all over the place in our house. And now I've got more space to build and display some new ones!'

All three boys laughed. 'Stay cool,' Michael told the brothers, and he left.

Chapter Twelve

In November 1967, as Alexander was nearing the end of his final year in primary school, his Aunt Mary died suddenly, leaving his cousins James and Tom orphaned. She had died of a stroke, and the Maclean adults knew that this had been induced by her heavy drinking. But they did not talk about it in front of the children, and Alexander and Roy only learned that their aunt, of whom they had been very fond, had had a rather serious drinking problem, once they were well into their adolescence. Alexander's memories of his aunt having always been accompanied by a bottle and a glass then took on a darker hue. But he had loved her: her expansive, generous, theatrical personality had appealed to him, and her fondness for the two Maclean brothers had been obvious to them both.

When Alexander first learned of Aunty Mary's death, one early afternoon on returning home from school, he had felt so shocked and distressed that he had burst into tears and run to his room and sat on his bed and cried for a while. His mother came to him after a little time had passed, and stroked his hair and patted his back, saying 'Aunty Mary did not suffer, you know. Her death was very sudden, and very quick.'

'What will James and Tom do, Mum?' he asked.

'I think we'll find that Aunty Mary left Hohenstein to your cousins, and that Aunty Margaret and Uncle William will stay on there and look after them. And they'll have Granny and Grandpa also – and us, of course. But you are right to feel concern for them, the poor boys. They're very young to have lost both their parents, and they'll need a lot of support and love.'

That night, alone in his bedroom after he had kissed his parents goodnight and said goodnight to Roy, Alexander brooded on this, the third death since the family had moved to Mallaig Road. The first had been Mrs. Irwin. Although she had been a stranger, her death had been traumatic for Alexander, because of the associations of guilt he felt. The second death had been his Grandpa Harry; and now Aunty Mary's death made three. And Alexander feared that all three deaths were in some fashion both a consequence of his own failings, and a judgement levelled against him. Alexander was too young to understand that the universal laws of cause and effect did not, after all, revolve around him, nor that bad things sometimes happened for no reason at all. He felt in some manner accountable for all three of these deaths. This conviction was utterly irrational, but all the more unshakable for it. He sat on his bed in his thin cotton summer pyjamas with their short pants, his elbows on his knees, and he brooded, and guilt and grief took hold of him. He would really miss Aunty Mary! He began to sob again.

His aunt's funeral was held at the Muizenberg cemetery. It was very warm. Alexander's mother dressed her sons in their carefully polished black school shoes and their grey slacks and white, long sleeved shirts, with ties. Alexander and Roy both shed some tears during the burial service, as did their father, Mary's brother, along with the Hohenstein residents Miss Spence-Traggart and Miss Grohen. Mary Scott's mother, Jeanie, wept also. So too did Tom, but James, like his grandfather, held himself rigid, his eyes dry, his face pale and grim. After the burial, the funeral-goers made their way to Rory's and Jeanie's home in Kommetjie, where a cold buffet lunch had been prepared by the maid, and Alexander found himself at a loss what to say to his cousins James and Tom. Granny Jeanie however gathered both these boys to her, and she kept them near her for the rest of the afternoon.

Only when he was home again, did it occur to Alexander that his grandparents had lost a daughter, and that they must be grieving terribly. He realised too that his father had lost a sister. He went up to his father, who was sitting in his armchair in the sitting room, staring at nothing.

'I love you, Dad,' he said.

His father smiled up at Alexander. 'I love you too, Sandy.'

The following Sunday the whole family met at Hohenstein. Granny Jeanie and Grandpa Rory were there, as were Aunty Margaret and Uncle William and their two little girls (for the Boyds would indeed be staying on at Hohenstein), and James and Tom of course were there. The family had lunch at Hohenstein (a private lunch, at which the five elderly long term residents were not present: they had their lunch in the guests' dining room), and afterwards, the four boys descended the steps from the wide veranda, and walked across the lawn towards the oak and pine woods and the stream, which at this time of the year was much reduced. James was very silent, but he had always been inclined to silences. Tom however displayed a slightly febrile cheerfulness.

'Let's build a dam across the stream,' suggested Alexander.

'If you want,' said James in a neutral tone.

'I'll help you, Sandy,' Tom said.

'And me,' Roy joined in.

So Alexander, Tom and Roy, having removed their shoes and socks, gathered large rounded river stones and began to arrange them across the flow of water, but James sat on a fallen tree nearby and simply watched the others, saying nothing.

In the late morning one Sunday in early December Mr. and Mrs. Maclean, with Alexander and Roy on the car's back seat, drove to Hohenstein. The Scott boys were to spend the rest of the day with the Maclean family. As a special treat, they were all to have lunch out. The Macleans, with their Scott cousins, drove along Rhodes Drive as it wound its way along the side of the mountain, Cape Town's eastern suburbs – Constantia, Bishopscourt, Kenilworth, Newlands, Rondebosch and Rosebank – spread out below them. They were headed for Rhodes Memorial, one of Alexander's favourite destinations, located on the eastern slopes of Devil's Peak. Here, the sense of elevation, of being situated high above the tens of thousands of people crowded in the suburbs below, brought Alexander a particular pleasure. He felt closer to the clear, lapis blue of the sky, which, except for the table cloth atop the mountain itself, was cloudless. He felt the sense of loss, of remorse and guilt, which seemed to afflict him so much of the time, recede, and blow away like smoke on the clean south-easterly wind.

Rhodes Memorial was a massive, weighty structure whose simple lines and beautiful proportions pleased Alexander's eye. It was built of Table Mountain granite, in the form of a Greek temple with Doric columns. The wide steps descending from the temple were flanked with great bronze recumbent lions, and Roy and Tom each clambered upon one of these lions, and sat astride them. The sculpture of the horse and its nude rider in bronze on its high stone plinth at the foot of the processional steps conveyed a very masculine energy and dynamism, as the horse's rider gazed towards the far mountain ranges of the African hinterland. James and Alexander stared for a while at the simple bronze bust of Cecil John Rhodes at the rear of the temple, in which the visionary and empire builder leaned on one elbow, a hand supporting his head, and what James was thinking, Alexander could not guess, but Alexander had been taught at school about the life and legend of this great, and (as he would one day appreciate) controversial man, during History lessons.

The Macleans, with their Scott cousins, then made their way to the restaurant, a simple, low building with a thatched roof, built of warm sandstone, and the boys smiled and laughed at the parrot with its bright plumage and intelligent, knowing eye, in its big cage outside the doorway. The family group sat at one of the wooden tables in the open air and looked at the printed menus. When a Coloured waiter came to take their orders, the four boys chose hamburgers, accompanied by milkshakes, with peach melba to follow. Mr. Maclean ordered a steak, and his wife chose line fish caught that morning, with spring potatoes and beans.

'Are you boys enjoying your meal?' Alexander's father asked.

'Yes thank you, Uncle Alex,' James replied.

'It's very nice, Dad,' Alexander responded. And it was. Alexander was enjoying his hamburger, and he was particularly partial to the fried onion rings. Alexander's appetite had recently increased considerably, and he had begun to gain noticeably in height – although not in bulk.

That afternoon the four cousins went to play at the stream flowing below the Maclean home. They walked to the end of Mallaig Road and all four boys removed their socks and shoes and splashed around in the water where the stepping stones crossed the stream. Alexander took his big toy cargo ship with him, and by loading its holds with a few of the smaller river stones, the boys worked out how to ballast it so that it floated evenly. James and Tom appeared to be enjoying themselves, and Alexander was glad: he had not forgotten what his mother had said about his cousins needing a lot of love now. The weather was typical of Cape Town in December. The sky was clear, the inverted bowl of the Heavens a perfect blue, and it was very warm, although it would have been even warmer had there not been a wind blowing. James alone was wearing long trousers – which he had rolled up to his knees.

'Oh – look!' Roy declared. 'Simba's come too!'

Simba the cat had appeared suddenly, and he miaowed loudly.

'Simba! What are you doing here?' Alexander asked the cat. The cat sat on the banks of the river and watched the children playing in the water. Alexander splashed through the water to the river bank with its thick green grass, and bent and picked Simba up. He wondered whether he should take the cat back home. But it was not far.

Hugging the cat, who purred, Alexander said 'I think it'll be alright if we let Simba stay with us, don't you, Roy?'

'Yeah – he should be alright.' So the Maclean brothers allowed their pet to watch them from the river bank. After a while they became engrossed in their play. The next time Alexander looked up to where the cat had been, he could not see him. He felt a momentary disquiet, then he put it out of his mind.

Simba turned up again, back home, later that afternoon. Alexander felt guilty that he had forgotten about the little creature. 'Oh Simba! You darling, where have you been?'

The cat miaowed, and rubbed its face against his cheek when Alexander bent and picked it up.

Mrs. Maclean served spaghetti bolognaise for an early supper, with plenty of grated cheese and lots of tomato sauce. All four boys thoroughly approved of the meal, and the two eldest, Alexander and James, ate exceptionally large helpings.

'It's delicious, Mum,' Alexander told his mother.

'Yes, Aunty Olivia, it is very nice,' James agreed.

'Well, I hope you'll have room for some jelly afterwards,' Mrs. Maclean said.

After supper, the four boys played snakes and ladders for a while, then Mr. Maclean and his sons drove James and Tom back to Hohenstein. It was by now growing dark, although the air still carried within it much of the warmth of the day. Alexander felt that sense of excitement that always accompanied drives in the dark, for they were rare treats. He and his brother were sitting in front on the wide bench seat with their father, with James and Tom on the back seat, and Alexander enjoyed looking at the Vauxhall's dashboard dials all lit up, glowing in the dark. The two younger boys – Roy and Tom – kept yawning during the drive. The Macleans did not linger at Hohenstein, and Alexander and Roy waited in the car while their father handed James and Tom over to their Aunt Margaret. Then the Macleans headed straight home. Alexander felt fairly sleepy by the time they reached home again. But it was too early to go to bed, so he found the book he was reading, *The Coral Island*, by R. M. Ballantyne (which had originally been published in the mid nineteenth century, although the edition he was reading, which had belonged to his maternal grandfather as a boy, dated from the late nineteenth century), and took it to the sitting room.

The two Maclean brothers loved Simba enormously. He was full of character, playful and affectionate. However, he could be rather independent at times, and some days he prowled in the bushes behind the house, wandering as far as the river. But he was always back home from his jungly adventures by six in the evening, for that was when Mrs. Maclean gave him his supper. The family tried to keep him indoors after his supper. He had never been permitted to go out adventuring at night. On the evening of Wednesday the 6th December, the cat had failed to come home by six. Nor was he home by seven. Alexander felt a sudden premonition of dread. It was as if a dark shadow had swept across his heart.

'Roy,' he said to his brother, 'I think we should go and look for Simba below the garden. Will you come with me?'

The two brothers climbed over the fence at the bottom of the garden and made their way through the bushes, calling 'Simba! Simba!' It was still daylight, just a few weeks short of the summer solstice. Roy forged ahead of his brother, who lost sight of him as he descended towards the stream. Then he heard Roy call 'Sandy!'

and there was something peculiar in the tone of his voice, and Alexander's sense of impending dread grew very strong. He pushed his way fast towards the stream, and he could see Roy, down by the edge of the water, below him.

'What's wrong?' Alexander asked. 'What have you found?'

His brother was making a sort of a moaning, keening sound, and Alexander burst through the last of the undergrowth by the banks of the stream, and he saw his brother crouched, the still body of Simba at his feet, surrounded by a scattering of river stones, clearly thrown there.

'Is he ... is Simba . . ?' Alexander asked.

Roy managed at last to speak. 'Simba is dead! Oh, Sandy – Simba is dead!'

Alexander bent and touched the still form of the cat, but he knew that the cat was dead. The position the body had assumed spoke of abandonment and death: the head was thrown back, the jaws were wide, the eyes wide open but glazed; there was a terrible absence of Simba himself from this still form. The horror Alexander had been anticipating for a long time was finally upon him.

Alexander scooped up Simba's broken body. He stood, weeping, then began to make his way back up the river bank and through the undergrowth, his brother, who was now wailing his grief and horror, close behind him. As if a long way away, Alexander heard his father calling for them. Mr. Maclean was waiting at the fence at the bottom of the garden, and Alexander handed him the broken body of the cat over the fence and turned to his brother. 'Can you climb over, Roy?'

The boys' father held the cat's body and looked with anguish at his sons' white, tear-streaked faces, and as they made their way up towards the house, Mr. Maclean called for his wife.

'Oh – my boys!' Mrs. Maclean exclaimed, as she met them at the kitchen door, and saw what her husband was carrying.

Mr. Maclean said 'They've found Simba's body. No – I don't know what happened.'

'I'm going to make you both drink some very sweet tea,' the boys' mother said, and she made her sons sit at the kitchen table. 'Alex!' she called to her husband. 'I think a touch of brandy in their tea – could you please bring the bottle of brandy?'

Mr. Maclean had laid Simba's body on the small table in the entrance hall, and he went to fetch the brandy from the drinks cabinet in the sitting room. While the two brothers, sobbing and gulping, were being tended by their mother in the kitchen, being made to drink their tea laced with brandy, their father wrapped the pathetic body of the cat in the cat's sleeping blanket, and took it through to the bedroom he shared with his wife, certain only that the boys must not have to see Simba's body again.

Mrs. Maclean put her sons to bed, and sat first with Roy, stroking his brow, until he was at last asleep, then went and joined her husband, who had been sitting with Alexander, who had also managed to fall asleep, the soporific effect of the brandy-fortified tea working on him also.

When Alexander awoke in the morning, it took several minutes before the horror of memory returned, followed immediately by sobs which began to shake his body.

'You boys can stay at home today, if you prefer,' their mother told them. Neither of her sons wished to go to school that day.

'Where is Simba now?' Alexander asked.

'His body is in our bedroom. But his soul is in Heaven now. He's happy, playing with other cats, and chasing butterflies.'

Round about mid morning Mrs. Maclean thought it might help her sons now if they were to bury Simba together. The two brothers helped their mother dig a grave about two and a half feet deep in one corner of the back garden, then Mrs. Maclean fetched the cat's body, wrapped in the blanket, and she laid it in the bottom of the grave. Then she began to fill in the grave, and the brothers helped her in this also. They were both weeping.

'We'll make a little headstone for him soon,' their mother said. 'God is looking after Simba now.'

The brothers wept and sniffled, and their mother stood with an arm around each of them by the graveside for a while, then she said 'We must remember all the happy times. Simba had a very happy life.' The three of them went inside.

How had the cat died? Both Mr. and Mrs. Maclean believed that the most likely explanation was that the friendly little animal had been lured close by a gang of boys from the Coloured community of Crawford across the *veld* on the far side of the Kromboom River, and then stoned to death. It seemed inconceivable that any of the Macleans' neighbours' sons would have killed their pet. But the brothers' parents did not share their thoughts with their sons. Who, anyway, talking with each other, had arrived at much the same conclusion. They did not see it as a race issue: they knew (as children generally know) that some children are very wicked indeed, and these particular wicked children most likely happened to be from the Coloured suburb across the *veld*.

Alexander would sometimes go and sit cross legged by the graveside for a while when he got back from school in the early afternoon, and tell Simba that he loved him, and that he was sorry. For he was afraid that Simba's death, like the three that had preceded it, must in some way have been necessary as a means to his further punishment.

The brothers went to school every day, and while Roy appeared to be recovering from his grief, Alexander once again withdrew into himself, and he became silent and uncommunicative. He could not rid his mind of the image of that abandoned, pathetic little corpse. At twelve years old – thirteen in two months' time – Alexander was old enough to fear that he could never be the same person again. But the school year was fast drawing to a close, and the end of year examinations loomed.

Since Stewart's departure Alexander had had no special friend. He no longer had a confidante at school. The other boys, put off by Alexander's brooding silences and by his expression, which was closed and unfriendly, so that he looked older than his years, left him alone. His classmates were anyway taken up with preparations for their end of year exams. Alexander knew that he must gain good marks if he was to be accepted by Rondebosch Boys' High, and he was counting on a new school, a new life, to bring to an end this period of suffering and retribution, so the immediacy of his grief for Simba began to fade as he began applying himself vigorously to revising for his end of year exams. He had realised suddenly that he had not much time left.

But Alexander's parents were concerned at how withdrawn their oldest son had become, and all they knew to do was to show as best they could that they loved him. Two weeks after the brothers had found Simba's body by the riverside, school broke up, and Alexander's primary school days were over.

Chapter Thirteen

Alexander's parents had had Graham Fellbridge and his wife to dinner twice, and they had been out to dinner two or three times with the Fellbridges in turn. During the Fellbridges' visits the conversation over dinner was general, with many Kenya reminiscences, for the Fellbridges, like the Macleans, had lived in Kenya. Alexander gathered that Mr. Fellbridge, like his father, had worked for an oil company in Kenya, and that he and his father had known each other then, although he did not remember the Fellbridges ever having visited the Macleans at their home in Nairobi. Alexander and Roy had been sent to bed after these late dinners, while the adults could be heard talking quietly in the sitting room. But Alexander was not surprised when, shortly before Christmas of 1967, his father told his sons over supper that the family would be moving to Johannesburg early in the new year. Alexander's astute, perceptive mind had already picked up that some major change was in the offing, some change in his life beyond his simply leaving primary school behind.

'I'm going into business with Graham Fellbridge. We'll have a factory in Johannesburg building tanker bodies and truck trailers.'

Mr. Maclean was a mechanical engineer, who had gained considerable experience at first in the storage, and later, in the road and rail transportation, of petroleum products. Graham Fellbridge likewise had gained much experience of petrol and oil tanker design. Mr. Fellbridge, now living in Cape Town, was planning to set up a company building trailers and tanker bodies – a range of tankers, not limited only to petrol and oil tankers – and once he heard that Alexander Maclean was also living in Cape Town, he had very quickly tracked him down, and proposed, over a dinner at which their wives were both present, that Alexander come in on the project, and invest a capital sum.

'It is primarily your experience in tanker bodies that I'm after, Alex. I have backers who will invest up to one hundred and fifty thousand Rand, but more capital would always be welcome, and if you were to bring a cash investment as well as your expertise, you would come in as a partner, rather than an employee.'

Alexander Maclean thought that he could scrape together a little over two thousand Rand. (To put this sum in perspective, the house at Mallaig Road had cost him fifteen thousand Rand).

'Two thousand Rand would be sufficient to get you a partnership, Alex. I would hold the position of CEO; you would be managing director.'

But Graham Fellbridge had told Alexander Maclean that he and his backers planned to build the factory in Johannesburg. 'Perhaps in time we'll open a factory in Cape Town, but Joburg is where the biggest market is.'

A year or two earlier, Alexander would have been distressed at the prospect of leaving Cape Town, but he felt he was ready to leave Cape Town now, and put an unhappy twelve months behind him. There was considerable appeal in making a fresh start in some new location. Roy however was less than happy.

'Oh Dad! I like it here! I wont have any friends in Johannesburg!'

'You'll soon make new friends, Roy,' his father told him.

'And we'll be able to have holidays in the game parks and in the Drakensberg.'

That Christmas, for Alexander, was an unhappy one. He grieved for Simba. The pathos of the little animal's death tore at his heart. He wondered whether he would ever be happy again.

Both Alexander and Roy were held back by their parents from beginning their new school year in Cape Town. The move to Johannesburg was imminent (a buyer for the house had been found): they would start their school year a little late in Johannesburg. In the second week of January, Mrs. Maclean, with the brothers in the back of the car, drove her husband to the airport, where he caught a flight for Johannesburg. He wished to look at the site for the new factory with Graham Fellbridge, and meet some of the Johannesburg backers, and he wanted to look at some of the houses that featured on the shortlist he and his wife had drawn up from the property section of the *Star*, the Johannesburg daily. He and Graham, who was also flying up to Johannesburg (Graham had already made a number of trips to Johannesburg during the preceding year) would be staying at the Balalaika Hotel in Sandton.

Alexander Maclean telephoned his wife from the hotel soon after checking in. Neither had a great deal to say, having seen each other only a few hours earlier, but Mr. Maclean said 'I miss you already, Livia.'

'I miss you too, Darling.'

'Give my love to the boys,' their father said at the end of the conversation.

He telephoned again early the following evening. He had found a house in the northern Johannesburg suburb of Blairgowrie, in the Randburg municipality. The neighbourhood was so new that there were houses still being built, and the street had only been tarred within the last year. The house had very recently been completed, the garden not yet laid out. It had a double garage, three bedrooms and a bedroom-sized study; a big sitting room and a separate dining room; an en suite bathroom and lavatory for the master bedroom, and another bathroom and lavatory also. The kitchen opened onto a small courtyard, which gave access to quarters for a live-in servant.

'We've looked at photos of the house, Darling,' Mr. Maclean told his wife. 'Do you remember it?'

'Yes, I do. We liked it, did n't we?'

They talked price and schools for a while. Then Mrs. Maclean said 'Well, I suppose you had better make an offer, Alex. We probably wont find anything better or more convenient.'

During the remainder of his extended holiday from school, Alexander read in the evenings, and drew and sketched, wishing to lose himself in fictional worlds and in the creations of his own hand. Some days he set off on his bike. He cycled further than he had ever cycled before, taking a lunchbox prepared for him by Dorcas, and staying out for entire mornings. Perhaps his mother failed to fully appreciate just how far he cycled.

Alexander made his way to Main Road in Rondebosch town centre, which in the past had represented the furthest extent of his exploration on his bicycle, and turning left into the busy Main Road (and his mother would surely have been horrified to have seen him), he cycled a short distance before turning right into Newlands suburb, glad to get off the busy road, which made him nervous. With the mountain now looming hugely in front of him, he made his way uphill towards Rhodes Drive, which he crossed via an underpass, entering Newlands Forest on the lower slopes of the mountain. None of the boys he knew from school had ever been so adventurous. The forest – cool, shaded, a refuge from the heat of high summer – delighted him. He used his bicycle lock to fasten the bicycle to the wooden fence at the edge of the parking ground, and he began following a walking trail through the forest.

The family's plans for a move to Johannesburg did not dismay

Alexander in the way they did his brother, Roy. Alexander had already had to say goodbye to his friend, Stewart, and there was no one special, outside his extended family, whom he would now miss. But the grandeur and drama, the breathtaking beauty of the Cape Peninsula's scenery, were to remain fresh in Alexander's memory for the next six years: the mountains, the forests and the ocean; those elements which defined the magical region encompassing the Cape Peninsula, the memory of which was to help Alexander endure what would be some rather unhappy years in high school. Until, having matriculated, he returned with his family to live in Cape Town once again.

The Maclean family visited Granny Jeanie and Grandpa Rory at Kommetjie one final time before their departure. Alexander's cousins, James and Tom were there, as were his Boyd relations. It was so warm that they took their lunch outside onto the *stoep*.

'Where will the boys go to school?' Alexander's grandmother asked his father.

'Roy will begin standard five at a primary school within walking distance of the house. Sandy will begin high school about four miles away. It's a new school: his is the first year there. Next year Roy will join him.'

'Dad,' Alexander asked, 'how will I get to school?'

'There's a school bus, I'm told, but maybe we'll buy a car for Mum, and she can drop you off and fetch you afterwards.'

Alexander did not like the idea of using a school bus. He had finished his lunch, and his appetite was not as robust as usual, so he declined pudding. Instead, he said 'I'm going for a walk.'

'Take your tray to the kitchen, Sandy,' his mother told him.

He did so, then set off down the path and out through the garden gate. Then he made for Long Beach, with the intention of walking far along the beach. He had only just realised that the family would be leaving the sea behind. He felt a sudden sadness at this thought. Then, as he saw Chapman's Peak rearing up to the north, with the massy bulk of Noordhoek Mountain to the north-east, he realised he had given no thought to living somewhere where there were no mountains. He no longer felt quite so sanguine at the prospect of moving to Johannesburg.

Alexander had made his way past the surfers and he was heading due north up the beach, with Chapman's Peak always in view in the distance. The tide was coming in. The sugary sand shifted beneath his feet. The Atlantic swell formed smooth, pale green rollers which grew steeper and were crested with white as they neared the beach, then they crashed with a roar and surged noisily up the sand, and every time they did so Alexander could feel the ground tremble beneath his feet. The water, translucent and foam flecked, then retreated with a hissing sound. The sky, a brilliant, pristine blue, was cloudless, and the south-easter cooled Alexander. After a while he sat on the sand and removed his shoes and socks, stuffing his socks into his shoes, and tying the shoe laces together and hanging the shoes around his neck. He enjoyed the sensation of damp sand between his toes, and the cold caress of the water on his calves when the tail end of a breaker reached out for him. He continued walking until there was no one else in sight, either before or behind him, and then he made his way up the dry, soft sand towards the dunes, where he leaned back against a sandy slope, and gazed at the sea.

He knew this was probably the last time he would be able to walk beside the sea. He felt sad and solitary. 'I'm the cat who walks alone,' he thought, thinking of the title of one of the stories in Rudyard Kipling's *Just So Stories* (*The Cat that Walked by Himself*); stories he had loved for as far back as he could remember.

This was true: Alexander had become a rather solitary boy. While he was not to remain solitary throughout his life – there would be periods of friendship and love and intense social activity – his solitary nature was to reassert itself many years hence as he stood before the gates of old age.

Chapter Fourteen

The distance by road between Cape Town and Johannesburg was almost nine hundred miles. During the first week of January Mrs. Maclean had begun packing. She had begged empty cardboard boxes from a number of local shops. Perhaps, after having made a move of several thousand miles between two countries just a few years earlier, a move which had included a sea voyage, the prospect of a relocation of a mere nine hundred miles, within the same country, did not seem daunting to Alexander's parents. On Wednesday the 17th January, the family said goodbye to Dorcas.

'Oh my boys, I will miss you!' Dorcas declared at the end of her final day at work. She hugged each brother in turn.

'We'll miss you too, Dorcas,' Alexander responded. Mrs. Maclean had written Dorcas an excellent reference, and as Dorcas was about to leave, Mr. Maclean handed her an envelope in which were twenty Rands. She had received her final wages earlier in the day.

'You must n't forget Paola,' the boys' father told them. 'Now is a good time to say goodbye to her.'

The brothers went next door and rang the doorbell. Paola herself answered the ring. She had a napkin in her hand, which she dabbed at her mouth. She must have been having an early supper.

'We wont see you tomorrow, Paola,' Alexander said. Paola would be at school when the Macleans left. 'We want to say goodbye.'

Paola, a lovely young woman now aged almost sixteen, shook Alexander's hand, and kissed him on the cheek. Then she grabbed Roy, her ardent admirer for three years, and hugged him. Roy was snuffling.

'Write to me!' she told him.

'I will,' Roy replied, wiping his tears with the back of his hand, but he never wrote to her.

'I wish we did n't have to say goodbye to people,' Roy told his brother, as they left Paola's home.

On the morning of Thursday the 18th January the big pantechnicon arrived at Mallaig Road, and the furniture, the stove (neither Kenya colonials nor South Africans called it a cooker), the fridge, the washing machine, and the many cardboard boxes packed by Mrs. Maclean, were loaded up. It was half past eleven before the lorry began its long journey inland, and after midday before the Macleans pulled out of their driveway in the old Vauxhall. The car was heavily laden with suitcases, bags, and a hamper packed with provisions for the one and a half day journey. Alexander's mother had also packed some children's books.

Had Simba lived, he would have accompanied the Macleans in the car.

'Say goodbye to Mallaig Road, boys. We're starting a new adventure!' Alexander's father declared.

Both boys turned in their seat and peered through the back window. 'Goodbye house,' Roy said.

'Goodbye Simba,' Alexander whispered.

Crossing the sandy Cape Flats was boring, Alexander thought. The landscape was flat and utterly uninspiring, and for many miles there was little of note to look at. There were few farms, due to the poor soil, and those few were hardscrabble affairs. But the distant Paarl Mountain, a huge granite outcropping, loomed closer and closer, and once the family had reached Paarl, the largest town in the Winelands, the countryside – bounded by dramatic mountains with towering peaks – struck Alexander as being far more interesting. Alexander and Roy were thrilled as the heavily laden car laboured up the narrow, winding, rock-girt Du Toit's Kloof pass through the mountains, and at the top of the pass their father stopped the car so that the engine could cool, and they gazed across the Cape Flats far below to the distant silhouette in miniature of Table Mountain. Alexander wondered when next he would look at that view. Beyond the pass lay the soaring Hex River Mountains, which in winter would be snow-capped, and the road followed the Hex River Valley, which was covered in a patchwork quilt of vineyards. Alexander was much taken by the dramatic, theatrical beauty of the region.

But by the time they reached the railway settlement of Touws River, the landscape had become dry and rocky, and the low hills that Alexander could now see were the colour of ash and clinkers. Beyond Touws River they began their long traverse of the Karoo, a region of stark, empty aridity, with hardly a sign of human life to be seen excepting only a rare windpump in the distance, or a huddle of green trees far away, watered by underground aquifers, amidst which would be found a farm house. This was a region given over to vast sheep ranches, viable only thanks to the windpumps which had first appeared around the mid nineteenth century. For mile after mile, the barbed wire strands of the boundary fences ran on either side of the road, and the telephone poles marched to the horizon. The road ran arrow straight with barely a deviation, towards an ill defined horizon shimmering with heat haze, and no matter how far they drove, that horizon was always many miles ahead of them. The temperature rose significantly. Mr. Maclean drove with his window wound down, for the illusion of coolness the oven hot passage of air gave him. There was not a worse time of day, nor a worse time of year, to cross the Great Karoo. The boys and their mother also had their windows wound partially down, and the heat and road noise became in time an assault on the senses.

The family reached the small town of Beaufort West in the late afternoon. The terrain was arid, semi desert, and it was still extremely hot. The Macleans would be spending the night here, at the Wagon Wheel Motel, and the brothers were overjoyed to escape the confines of the hot, noisy car. The noise of the buffeting of the hot air and the drumming of the tyres on the road through their open windows had been exhausting. They ran wildly around the motel's grounds, shouting happily at one another; there was a sparse, patchy lawn and hardy desert proof shrubs. The family had covered a third of the distance of their journey.

The Macleans ate a good breakfast in the motel's restaurant in the morning, and were on the road again by half past eight. This was the best time of day to cross the Karoo. The air did not yet feel as if it was coming from the open door of a furnace. The family reached the town of Colesberg on the far side of the Great Karoo around half past eleven, and thereafter the landscape began subtly to change. There were more stands of trees, and more patches of green. Signs of human habitation became more and more commonplace. The Macleans ate lunch at a roadhouse outside Bloemfontein, and used the lavatories. As they had done the previous afternoon, they pulled the car over at a roadside picnic spot round about four in the afternoon. There was a sturdy, concrete table painted white with a white painted concrete bench either side of it, partially shaded from the sun by some pepper trees which were bedecked with clusters of tiny pink false peppercorns. Here Mrs. Maclean produced warm but wonderfully refreshing *naartjies*, and somewhat unpalatable sandwiches that were more than a day old, along with hot, sweet, milky coffee in a thermos which the motel kitchen had prepared, and some orange squash for the boys.

It was after nine-thirty that evening before the Macleans reached Johannesburg, and after the long, almost empty road, and the sparsely inhabited terrain of their journey, the huge sprawl of Johannesburg and the busy Friday night traffic and bright city lights came as something of a shock to the brothers, both of whom had fallen asleep, and woke, blinking at the noise and lights. It was with enormous relief shared by all that Mr. Maclean, whose temper had been growing rapidly shorter as a number of wrong turnings were made, managed at last (with his wife trying to navigate from the map of Johannesburg she held open on her lap, the saloon roof light turned on) to find the hotel in the tree lined Tyrwhitt Avenue in Rosebank, a shopping and residential suburb to the north of Johannesburg, where they were to spend the remainder of the night. It was by now after ten-thirty, and there was a night porter only on duty at the hotel desk, but he took pity on the bedraggled travellers and went and made Mr. and Mrs. Maclean some tea.

The Macleans had passed the furniture lorry near Paarl, but it had overtaken them again while they overnighted at the Wagon Wheel Motel. It was again passed by the Macleans that following Friday afternoon, and was due to deliver its contents to the new house in Blairgowrie the next morning. And just before Mrs. Maclean, exhausted, fell asleep by her husband's side in the hotel bed, she thought 'I must remember to buy food and groceries tomorrow before the shops close at one …'

Chapter Fifteen

Alexander turned thirteen the following month. He was no longer a little boy, but a teenager. He spent the next five years at a high school which, when he joined it, had only just opened its gates to its first intake of students, beginning with standard six only. The school was located in Bryanston, a moneyed suburb of large houses and even larger plots of land. There was open countryside not far from the school; grassland for the most part, but there were one or two commercial market gardens still in operation. The school consisted of a concrete and brick block of classrooms on three floors, and a quadrangle, on one side of which were the administrative offices, and on another the school hall and the gymnasium. The grounds were extensive, with playing fields, cricket pitches and tennis courts, and were planted with *Schotia Brachypetala*, or weeping boer-bean trees, and jacarandas. The headmaster and his staff would be creating school traditions from scratch, and this they were to do with a studied care, consciously modelling these traditions on those of a British public school. A majority of the school's pupils came from well to do families, and the school was not short of money.

Alexander would sometimes wander down to the far side of the twin rugby fields during the longer, second break. The vast expanse of lawn was planted with tough, hard wearing, quick growing Kikuyu grass. It was an environment favoured by the hoopoe birds which the school had adopted for the crest on its blazer badges and on its letter head. Alexander liked to watch the hoopoe birds as they probed busily in the lawn with their beaks, their crests bobbing up, erect, like the war crests favoured by Mohican warriors in story books he had read. Before Alexander had completed his five years at the school, an Olympics size swimming pool, with changing rooms, tiered benches along one side, and a covered pavilion on the other, had been built in the grounds.

Within his first few weeks at school, Alexander, who was not usually very good at making friends, had made two friends who were to remain with him right through high school. Alexander was to make no other close friends at school; equally however, he was to make few enemies. Like Alexander, these two friends were the sons of immigrants. Both were English boys, one the son of middle class parents from the south of England, the other (to whom Alexander was more closely drawn) a Lancashire working class boy whose father had made good in South Africa. This boy's accent was unashamedly North Country proletariat, and Alexander found it appealing.

'Come on Phil – please say "muddy pup" for me,' Alexander would tease his friend.

Philip would grin in response. 'Moody poop,' he would answer – or at least that was how it sounded to Alexander's ears.

'You're a good honest chum,' Alexander would tell him.

'You mean "choom," Sandy,' Philip would reply. Then both boys would burst into laughter. This discovery of a close friend at school had been a special and unexpected blessing for Alexander, and did much to make him a far more cheerful boy than he had been during his last year or so in Cape Town. His friendship with Philip in particular helped him to outgrow the guilt he had felt whenever he had thought of old Mrs. Irwin's death, or the deaths of his grandfather, his Aunt Mary, and the family's darling pet Simba. Alexander no longer brooded on these unhappy but ultimately quite ordinary and unrelated acts of God. He was growing up.

English and Scottish surnames abounded at the school: the former a mix of first generation immigrant families (like those of Alexander's two friends) and of longer established families of English origin, some of them reaching back to the 1820 Settlers, the founders of the English presence in the then Cape Colony. The Scottish surnames belonged to children whose forebears (like Alexander's own family in Kenya) had emigrated from Scotland in most cases several generations earlier. There were few Afrikaners at the school, but there existed a small number of children from wealthy Johannesburg Jewish families. Year by year, Alexander remained in the senior year, moving up a form each year, as a new intake of school pupils arrived in the increasing number of forms beneath him.

The student body was divided by academic streaming: A stream, B stream and C stream. The children in A stream were being readied for university entrance; those in B stream might continue to technical college; but those in C stream completed their education two years earlier than the others, leaving school at the end of standard eight, and they were not destined for higher education at all. From their ranks would be drawn the junior functionaries of local government, and society's tradesmen – mechanics, carpenters, plumbers, and so forth – whose job training would take the form of apprenticeships. Alexander and his friends were of course all three in the A stream, and it was understood that they would be continuing to university after they had matriculated. There were at first only two A stream classes in the senior year, broadly divided between those boys who had elected to study Latin, and those who, like Alexander, had chosen French.

'I was a complete duffer at Latin at school,' Alexander's father had told him. 'I struggled to make any sense of it.'

Alexander's mother (whose own mother, born and raised in France, had taught her to speak French) advised him 'French will be so much more useful to you, Sandy, and I may be able to help you.'

When he grew up Alexander was to find that he had a flair for languages. He was to visit Paris and the south of France several times, and with each visit his schoolboy French improved. Alexander was to particularly enjoy speaking French, a language he associated with all the European civilised values. Along with Afrikaans, he was to speak it if not fluently, then competently. Paris, during each visit he made, engaged Alexander's emotions. It was a glorious, dramatic city, a cityscape of great beauty. By the late nineteen-nineties Alexander was to find that he had outgrown his earlier passion for Britain and for all things British; he sometimes found himself wishing that he had been born a Frenchman, rather than a Briton. But these passions lay in the future: for now he enjoyed his studies of French at school, and it became one of his favourite subjects.

'*Que dit Balzac de la société française de l'époque?*' the rather glamorous young French teacher would ask the class, after having read a passage from *Le Père Goriot*, a novel by Honoré de Balzac that the class was studying at the time. Her questions, couched in French, would invariably be met by a profound silence from the class, but sometimes Alexander felt he dared hazard a reply, and he would hastily formulate a response in halfway acceptable French, and *Mamselle* would smile at him as he spoke.

'*Oui, c'est exact! Bien!*' she would respond, and Alexander would bask for a while in her favour and in the grudging admiration of his classmates.

Yet in years to come, Alexander was to regret his ignorance of Latin. His interest in Latin was first piqued through his interest in the historical Catholic Church, and in the Latin liturgy of the Mass. He became aware that Latin was not entirely the dead language he had always thought it to be. The definitive texts of the Church's official documents and encyclicals were written in Latin. Latin was still used as a *Lingua Franca* on rare occasions in the Church, although the days when the majority of educated men, and all churchmen, could speak Latin, and Latin could commonly be used as a bridge language, were over. Italian, and then English, were the languages of the Vatican today.

Over time Alexander made an effort to teach himself some Latin. He found this exercise challenging, but his mind appreciated the wonderful, iron-clad logic and rationality of the language's structure, and he came to understand why a grounding in Latin taught one how to think. Some of the Biblical passages with which he was familiar, such as the verses from Alexander's favourite Psalm, Psalm 51, seemed to him to be imbued with particular spiritual resonance when recited in Latin.

"Sacrificium Deo spiritus contribulatus; cor contritum et humiliatum, Deus, non despicies."*

During his final two years at school, the distinction between those pupils who had chosen to take Science and Geography for Matric, and those like Alexander who were studying Biology and History, created further divisions in years nine and ten, creating an additional class in each. As a consequence, the classes in standards nine and ten became smaller, and the tuition was more personalised.

Alexander's friend Philip (the boy whose home in Manchester had had an outside lavatory) remained in the same class as Alexander, and continued to be his closest friend. Robin, his other

---

*   The sacrifices of God are a broken spirit: a broken and a contrite heart, O God, thou wilt not despise.

English friend, was studying Latin, and he had chosen Science for his final two years, and as a consequence, Alexander saw less of him at school, although, like Philip (who lived not far from the Macleans), Robin sometimes visited Alexander's home after school during the summer months, ferried there and back by his mother in a Volvo station wagon, where he spent the remainder of the afternoon by the large swimming pool that the Macleans had had built in their garden. During the summer the boys were very brown, and their tans never entirely wore off during the short wintertime. Roy too had his school friends visiting, and some afternoons there might be five or six boys playing in the swimming pool. They were fed sandwiches, and sometimes cake and cookies, by Mrs. Maclean, and given orange juice or Coca-Cola to drink. The suburbs when Alexander was young rang with the sound of children's shouts and laughter. South African society was still a young society.

Alexander was to remain in touch with both Philip and Robin for another three years or so after leaving school, but by then the Macleans were once again living in Cape Town, and over time, Alexander lost touch with both these school friends. As late as Alexander's seventh decade, however, Philip, Alexander's closest friend throughout his high school years, still intruded sometimes in his dreams as he lay asleep at night.

Philip was good at PT, especially gymnastics, his India rubber body hurling its way through the exercises with a casual confidence and abandon which Alexander envied and admired. Alexander himself thoroughly loathed PT classes, in particular gymnastics. It seemed to him that the risk of crippling himself permanently during this period at school was very high. Nor did he enjoy the sweaty, hyper masculine locker room atmosphere before and after PT class, with its talk of girls and sex, and he felt that his skinny body compared poorly with the often well formed bodies of his class mates. He was to become intensely self conscious during his final two years at high school, horribly aware of his scrawny build, and afflicted by confused yearnings which seemed to him to be both illicit and unnatural.

Nor did Alexander enjoy cricket in the summertime. He never came to grasp the rules of the game. He continued to play tennis through the winter; those Highveld winters, dry, filled with sunshine, but desperately cold at night. He felt no great love for tennis, but nor did he hate it as he did PT classes. And tennis got him out of having to play soccer or rugby, sports for which he showed no aptitude whatsoever.

What Alexander enjoyed most was wintertime cross-country. The school was still adjacent to large tracts of open countryside, and with his low body mass and long legs, Alexander was built for long distance running. At an inter-house meet early on a Saturday morning, the Highveld winter sun would not yet be very far above the horizon as the runners set off; the ground in the shade was still brittle and crackling underfoot with the night's thick frost. The air on Alexander's bare arms and legs was bracing: dry and sharp. Alexander would set off quite fast for the first mile or so of the four mile run (the races were run by boys from standards eight, nine and ten), but not quite as fast as many of the other boys. However, after the first mile or two had been completed, he would forge steadily ahead of those who had earlier left him behind, and be among the first ten, sometimes the first five, at the finishing line. Once or twice he finished the race in the first three. Alexander gloried in his strength and stamina, and he felt the deepest pleasure as he overtook one boy after another. This – unlike PT, unlike gym, unlike team sports – was something he could excel in! His asthma troubled him less and less frequently as he grew older. These races helped too to reaffirm Alexander's seniority in his brother's eyes. Despite Roy by now being bigger and taller than his older brother, Alexander always beat him at cross-country. He consistently came in ahead of his friend Philip, too.

'I wish … I could run … like you … Sandy,' Philip panted after one race, as he came in some time behind Alexander.

'You're not skinny enough! Anyway, I'ld rather be good at gym.'

Anxieties other than PT arose during Alexander's final two years at school. He was sixteen years old, a standard nine pupil, when one afternoon after class, sitting with Philip on a bench alongside the rugby fields (there to cheer on Robin, who was in the rugby first team, and the school, as they played a visiting rugby team), Alexander had become suddenly intensely aware of how well shaped his friend's hands were: they were strong, fine, subtle in their form, and browned by the sun. In the days and weeks that followed, Alexander was at times very conscious of his friend's physical presence. He had no frame of reference within which to understand what he might be feeling. He could barely define what he was feeling. He was left only with a sense that he was incurably sinful, and that if others even guessed at his confusions and uncertainties and wicked, secret thoughts, he would be mocked and reviled, for *moffies*, the slang term for homosexuals, were universally mocked and persecuted at school.

Poor Alexander. The guilt and unhappiness he felt were pronounced. Matters were made worse during one session of the boys' weekly "Guidance" class.

'Most of you are sixteen or seventeen years old now,' their teacher said. 'How many of you have not yet kissed a girl?'

Nobody raised his hand.

'If you have n't yet kissed a girl by your age, there's something wrong with you. Your sexuality is askew.'

Oh, the damage that can be done to young people by foolish and malicious adults! These words were to stick in Alexander's memory for the rest of his life.

Alexander dared approach neither a teacher nor his parents for advice in this matter, so he visited a Catholic priest one afternoon after school, at the Catholic church a few miles from their home.

Robin was a Catholic. He had been talking about the sacrament of confession in the Catholic Church. Alexander was convinced that he was caught in the grip of sin, and that perhaps, if he confessed something he could barely even put a name to, he might be set free from that sin's hold over him.

The priest, an Irishman in his forties, listened to Alexander as he struggled to express his fears, and his conviction that he was trapped by sin.

'You're not to worry, Alexander,' the priest told him. 'Many boys go through this sort of phase at about your age. You'll almost certainly outgrow it.'

But Alexander did not believe he would outgrow what he felt when he gazed out of the corner of his eye at Philip's trim form.

Alexander's final two years at high school were not, on the whole, happy years. He felt increasingly isolated and alienated, a creature burdened with a secret he dared not reveal. He began to seek out solitude, much as he had aged twelve, and he spent less time with Philip and Robin. Afternoons with Philip by the poolside at home were no longer as enjoyable as they had once been, for the sight of Philip's tanned body, and the subtle play of the muscles on his wet torso, shining in the sun, caused Alexander too much disturbance of mind.

Alexander began walking home by himself after school some afternoons, spurning the lifts home by car which his mother (who was now working mornings in town, and was only home by two) had arranged for his brother and himself with neighbours' sons attending the school. With the pass laws savagely policed (which meant that black people in South Africa had to carry an identity document, a "pass", confirming their right to be present in a particular district or region), Alexander would not meet any black people, until he had regained the suburbs, when he might see the occasional female domestic servant walking to or from the shops on her *madam's* business.

Alexander valued this time alone, as he walked across the several miles of *veld* and open countryside which lay between the school and Blairgowrie suburb, and which consisted of grassland dotted with a few trees – Scots pine, blue gum, and the occasional indigenous acacia. The Highveld sky was vast; an azure canvas across which fat cumulus clouds drifted on a summer's afternoon, and in the winter it was an inverted bowl of completely cloudless blue, darkening by imperceptible degrees to cobalt directly overhead. Although there was little wildlife of any size left in the district, there were rodents and a wealth of insects. Some of the latter were enormous and very striking: there were brilliantly coloured giant grasshoppers, their carapaces gleaming like bright colourful enamel, and huge beetles, some decorated with horns. There were snakes too, and sometimes Alexander, who trod lightly, would see a snake, usually one of the harmless variety he thought of as grass snakes or mole snakes, but once or twice he saw a puff adder, with its diamond-patterned back, and once he saw a very poisonous rinkhals, which he later identified (paging through a book on South African snakes in the school library) from the two broad white bands across the chest near the top of its dark grey body, as it reared and spread its hood. Alexander instinctively took several steps back from the rearing serpent. He was to learn from the reference book on snakes he had found that the rinkhals spat its venom, which, like that of the puff adder, was cytotoxic and caused severe tissue damage. Alexander was not at all fond of snakes, but he was nonetheless thrilled when he spotted one, evidence of a natural order not yet utterly crushed and tamed by Man.

Alexander's mother was by then working half days at the *Star*, Johannesburg's big daily. Mrs. Maclean was relieved of the necessity to do the housework, for there was a live-in maid (she had her own quarters accessed via the small kitchen courtyard), a black woman named Thina, whom Mrs. Maclean trusted enough to work unsupervised until she returned home at about two in the afternoon. Olivia Maclean's sons were no longer as dependent on their mother as they had been when they were younger. They had lives of their own now, and they shared less with their mother. There were times when she felt that her sons had secrets they kept from her. She felt this in particular with her eldest son. Her husband spent less time at home than he had when the family was young. He worked late. He frequently met customers for drinks in the evenings in one of the fashionable hotel bars. So Olivia Maclean sought to compensate for the troubling emptiness and loneliness of her life, by working half days at the newspaper.

The newspaper's seven-storied office building and printing works took up an entire block in the Johannesburg city centre. Mrs. Maclean caught a bus into town in the early mornings (driving during the rush hour was no pleasure), and she was home again by two o' clock. She had had a car of her own for some years now, and for a while she had been carrying and fetching her sons (along with the occasional schoolmate) to and from school most week days, but her sons shared lifts in schoolmates' cars now. She combined administrative work at the newspaper with an occasional journalistic submission of her own. These comprised either wry suburban social commentaries, or curious stories from Johannesburg's past, and the *Star* was always happy to run them.

'You're a clever girl,' her husband told her. 'I knew it was more than just your pretty face I was drawn to when I began courting you.'

Mrs. Maclean smiled at her husband, who, home early for a change, had been reading his wife's latest piece in the *Star*. She bent and kissed his cheek. 'You can be quite the charmer when you put your mind to it, Alex Maclean.'

Chapter Sixteen

Alexander sat his Matric exams towards the end of the school year in 1972. He stayed home the odd morning if he was not writing an exam that day, busy revising, alone but for Thina, and Lulu, the Siamese cat, who had been with the family since 1968. Alexander was seventeen years old, a year younger than many of his peers. Only Maths proved truly challenging for him. Indeed, he was barely able to scrape a pass mark in Mathematics, and this was to prevent him from being accepted by the university's architectural faculty. Nor could he any longer consider joining Safmarine, the South African merchant marine operator, as a cadet officer. For a couple of weeks after he received his Matric results, he felt lost: his dreams of studying architecture, or of going to sea as a bridge officer, had been dashed.

'I don't know what to do now!' he exclaimed during supper one evening.

Alexander's mother said 'You have always loved History. Why don't you take History at university?'

'Yes, but what would I do with a History degree, Mum?'

'A great many careers are open to humanities graduates, Sandy. Jobs where they are more interested in proof that you have a brain and can think, than in what exactly you studied at university,' his mother responded. 'Or perhaps,' she continued, 'you could become an academic at university. You could study for your master's degree, and become a History lecturer.'

Mr. Maclean had kept silent. He had two sons to put through university, and he felt that a financial investment in Roy – who knew exactly what he wished to be; he wished to become a mechanical engineer – would likely pay dividends in excess of Alexander's studying History. Accordingly, he and his wife spoke to the school's headmaster, who told them that if Alexander was to study History and French at university, he could obtain a bursary from the Transvaal Education Department. An urgent application was duly forwarded by the Head on Alexander's behalf to the TED (urgent, because the university year commenced in early March), and some telephone calls were made, and Alexander was awarded a bursary for study towards a Bachelor of Arts in History and French. The bursary covered his university academic fees, and unless it was repaid in full after he had graduated, he would have to work it off with three years spent working as a teacher for the TED. Alexander could barely imagine ever possessing the self confidence needed to take charge of a classroom of high school pupils. He was in fact never to have to do so.

Most of the boys from his Matric class at school threw themselves wholeheartedly into their new found freedoms at university, conducting extremely busy social lives, and in some cases experimenting with illicit substances to which they had had almost no access while at school. Although they too were at university, Alexander found that he saw much less of Philip or Robin than he had at school, and he made no close friends that first year at university. He joined no clubs or societies. In the sole expression of his new found independence, he (like many of the other boys who had been at school with him) grew his hair longer. Within a few months, Alexander was wearing his straight, thick golden hair in a pageboy cut, and although he had little real awareness of how fresh faced and innocent, how wide eyed and appealing, he looked, he did possess some vanity: he lavished attention upon his hair, washing it frequently and treating it with conditioner after each wash.

Alexander did not join the other first years he had been at school with when they drank at the bar in the sports pavilion. Unlike Philip and Robin, he was not asked to their weekend parties. One or two fellow students on the courses he was studying made friendly overtures to Alexander, but he spurned almost all these approaches. No, Alexander, very much like the cat in Rudyard Kipling's *Just So Stories*, kept to himself. It was almost as if he was harbouring his energies.

Alexander was to spend only one year at university before putting his studies on hold indefinitely. The break came naturally, for in October 1973 Alexander's father and Graham Fellbridge decided to open a small factory in Cape Town, and Mr. Maclean was to oversee this operation. The Maclean family moved to Cape Town in late January of 1974, where Alexander, who had caught a flight to Cape Town two weeks ahead of the family's move, and had been staying with his grandparents at Kommetjie, rejoined them. The Macleans had left Cape Town six years earlier. Alexander did not apply to the University of Cape Town to continue his degree. His father repaid the year's tuition fees outstanding to the Transvaal Education Department. Roy registered as a first year engineering student at the University of Cape Town. He too had begun to grow his hair.

'My handsome boys!' Mrs. Maclean exclaimed one day, when the two brothers (Roy even taller than Alexander, who measured six feet and two inches in height) happened to be standing alongside each other.

'Oh Mum …' Roy responded. Alexander grinned and glanced modestly towards his shoes.

Alexander was far happier living in Cape Town than he had been in Johannesburg. The topography, mountainous and full of visual drama with its backdrop of limitless ocean, with much of the mountain slopes clad in dark pine forests, and wreathed in mists and cloud in the winter, brought him joy, as did the views of the boundless shining sea with its infinite horizons. There was much more wildlife to be seen. Colourful sunbirds, tiny shining creatures, flitted from flower to flower as they sipped nectar from the proteas and other wild flowers on the mountain slopes. Alexander came across troops of baboons when he was hiking in the mountains, and he sometimes saw small antelopes – in particular, the Cape grysbok – and other creatures. One late afternoon in early winter, on the Back Table, not far from the head of Skeleton Gorge (which Alexander planned to descend rapidly, reaching the car park at Kirstenbosch Gardens before it grew dark), he saw movement out of the corner of his eye. He was sitting silently and still on a boulder, admiring the view across the suburbs of Newlands and Bishopscourt which lay far below. He could see across the Cape Flats, to the distant barrier of mountains, topped with early snow which gleamed white where errant rays of the westering sun broke through the cloud cover. Alexander cast his gaze on the spot where he had noticed movement, and he could hardly believe what he was seeing.

'Oh my gosh,' he breathed softly to himself. 'Oh my gosh.'

Alexander felt an access of joy and wonder, as he watched a caracal cat, a creature not dissimilar to a European lynx in build, as it crossed an open patch of rocky ground about forty feet from him. Its gait was fluid and full of grace. Its coat was red gold, and its large ears each had a long tuft of fur on the tip. The animal – such a rare sighting on Table Mountain! – turned its head and looked at him, then it suddenly bounded forward and within an instant it was gone from sight.

Alexander had attained his Cape Peninsula hiker's apotheosis.

During his final year at school, and at university, Alexander had often dreamed of going abroad as soon as he was able; of spending a lengthy working holiday in Britain – and possibly, even further afield. (But his achievement of this latter ambition was to have to wait a few years). He had become conscious at some level that if he was to overcome the traumas of late adolescence, and allow his somewhat repressed personality to blossom, he must wrench himself free from the known and the familiar, and travel far from home. He wished in fact to reinvent himself. He felt that there would be more opportunity to do so overseas for someone like himself, than then existed in South Africa's rather provincial society; a society that still owed more to the social conventions of the 1950s than it did to those of the early 1970s. But he did not for a moment imagine that he could simply ask his father to fund his travels; no, he knew that he would have to find a job and save up the money he would need.

And so Alexander joined the in-store management training course at one of Cape Town's well known retail concerns, reporting for duty in mid February, not long after his paternal grandmother, Jeanie Maclean, had died. The training course had begun a month earlier, but Alexander's family had only arrived in Cape Town in late January. They moved into a hotel in Rondebosch. With Granny Jeanie's passing Alexander had lost the second of his grandparents. He cried when she died. He had always loved Granny Jeanie, and he had grown even closer to her during the two weeks he had stayed with his grandparents in Kommetjie, ahead of the rest of his family moving to Cape Town.

The Maclean family's new home was in Constantia, a sprawling, moneyed suburb below the Back Table, where the plots were much bigger and the houses were much larger than those of the Rondebosch of Alexander's childhood.

'How frightfully posh,' Mrs. Maclean commented, tongue in cheek, the first time she was shown the house.

Her husband laughed. 'We can afford it, Darling.'

They had bought a newly built house again – the Macleans' third newly built house in South Africa. This house was much bigger than their house in Johannesburg had been, and although it had only four bedrooms (one of which, the master bedroom, had its own paved patio looking onto the garden, and an en suite bathroom and lavatory, with a separate dressing room), there was also a guest suite, with a bathroom and WC attached, which the Macleans would find useful when relations from abroad visited periodically. There was a big entrance hall, with an adjacent WC and a closet for coats. The remaining three bedrooms shared a bathroom and a lavatory between them. There was also a study; a dining room; a sitting room with a fireplace (a paved patio, with a varnished hardwood pergola above it, which Mrs. Maclean would use to support two bougainvillea plants, opened off the sitting room, overlooking the walled garden); a den (as Mr. Maclean called it) with a fireplace of its own; a big fitted kitchen; a pantry with a double sink; a larder with cupboards and shelves; and a laundry room. On the far side of the kitchen courtyard were located a box room and quarters for two live-in servants. There was a double garage, communicating with the kitchen courtyard. The property comprised half an acre – twice the size of the property in Blairgowrie – and the garden was almost entirely surrounded by a high brick wall, against which Mrs. Maclean would in time grow golden shower, honeysuckle and jasmine. A mature oak tree grew in the garden, and Mrs. Maclean bought a sturdy wooden bench, which Roy sanded down and varnished, to place beneath it.

Within three days Lulu, the family cat, was at home in the new property. Watching her exploring the pantry, the larder and the laundry room for the second time, Alexander laughed and called to his brother, who was mending a loose cupboard door hinge in the kitchen, 'Roy! It's so funny watching Lulu as she tries to work out how these rooms relate to the rest of the house.'

'I wonder what part of the house will become her favourite?' Roy responded.

In fact, unless during the day time she was lying outside in the sun in the garden, or she was seeking privacy (in which case a bedroom would do) she was to favour the den, for the sitting room, although smartly furnished and decorated, remained largely unused by the family unless they had visitors.

Alexander's Aunt Margaret sold him her car, a 1964 Triumph Herald 1200, which she had owned since new. This was Alexander's first car, and he grew to love it. His father named the car Betsy, after his own first car, and the name stuck. Alexander had a weekday off work once a fortnight (he usually chose a Friday), on top of his one and a half days every weekend, to compensate him for having to work Saturday mornings, and he explored the Cape Peninsula on weekends and during his weekdays off work. Alexander had discovered a deep and abiding happiness in hiking in the mountains, and he would park his car as near as possible to the start points of a wide variety of mountain hikes. This sometimes meant that he would have to drive along narrow, single track forestry reserve roads for some distance. He came across few other people in the mountains, particularly during the week. Alexander experienced a sublime joy in these wild, high places, where, with each turn in the trail, a fresh vista of extraordinary beauty would present itself.

There was a young man named Richard on the training course with Alexander, who shared with him his love for the mountains. He was a good looking, dark young man with a self contained air, a year older than Alexander, and he was the closest Alexander had to a real friend at work. Sometimes these two young men would set out on a day's hike in the mountains together.

'Are you still planning on going overseas next year, Rick?' Alexander asked him, as they were ascending the Smuts Path to the Back Table in the early summer of 1975.

'*Ja*, probably in March or April,' Richard replied. 'It'll be springtime in Britain. I'd like to work in London, but I want to visit Europe too.'

'So do I!' Alexander declared enthusiastically. 'I have relations in Berkshire, but I'd like to live and work in London.'

The trail was steep, and there was no cover from the hot sun. The ground was hard and rocky, but Alexander loved the Mountain, and he was very fit. He was not even breathing hard. He stopped however, and turned to admire the view. The suburb of Bishopscourt, with its many trees, its grand houses and big gardens, already lay far below them. He could see across the Cape Flats to the distant mountains, a jagged grey-blue line against the horizon. There lay a great sweep of distant False Bay in view, the water a brilliant blue, and beyond its farthest shore were more mountains. The two young men were alone now, having earlier overtaken a party of four hikers. It was warm and still, as there was no wind in the gorge. The sun was high in the sky, for they had only set off from Kirstenbosch car park at about a quarter to eleven. The two companions stared at the view.

'I plan to leave South Africa in January or February next year,' Alexander said. 'We must stay in touch, Rick.'

'We will, Sandy. It'll be a *jorl* travelling in Europe together in the summer.'

'I'll give you my aunt's address and phone number in England. She'll know how to contact me.'

'OK.' Richard turned and set off up the trail again. Like Alexander, he was wearing shorts, a tee shirt, and hiking boots. He was very brown. Alexander was happy to follow in his path for a while.

For the most part, Alexander hiked alone, and because he loved the mountains and the creatures he might see in them, he did not feel lonely. In the mountains of the Cape Peninsula Alexander experienced a communion with the natural world, a communion he was to reaffirm, in both the northern and southern hemispheres, right through his life. Walking in an environment where there was a complete absence of man-made sounds, where the signs of Man's presence were few, brought soul's ease to Alexander.

Alexander delighted in the wild flowers of the mountains, in particular the red disa, that orchid emblematic of Table Mountain, but he loved the Watsonias, the multi-floreate ericas, the wild iris, and of course the King Protea, South Africa's national flower, no less. He derived great pleasure from watching the flashing sunbirds as they flitted from blossom to blossom, their bright plumage shining in the sun like jewelry. The harsh barking of a troop of baboons reaffirmed for Alexander that this mountainous environment, lying so close alongside Cape Town's urban sprawl, was a wild one, hardly touched by Man. Alexander knew where the year round springs were located, where he could obtain clear, clean water to drink no matter how baking the summer season. Even during the short winters he would be up in the mountains in the cold, often wet, weather at every opportunity, wearing a heavy pullover, corduroy trousers, a scarf, a waterproof windcheater and a woolen beanie on his head. He came to know the mountain trails so well that even when the cloud came down and he could see no further than fifteen feet ahead, he did not fear losing his bearings.

Alexander gained experience working in three separate retail departments in the store during his first year's training. He spent the final three months of 1974 being trained up to take over from a department manager and buyer when she left in the new year to have a baby. In January 1975 Alexander, still aged only nineteen, was appointed a department manager and buyer. He was immensely proud of his gold lapel badge – an indication that he had joined the ranks of management. He was earning more too.

'Thanks Dad,' he said, when his father congratulated him on his early promotion to management. 'But it's not really very hard. My old ladies actually run the department.'

Alexander had a full time sales staff of three middle aged white women of long service and much experience, with a youngster in addition joining the team on Saturday mornings.

On what did Alexander spend his salary? He paid the largest share into his savings account each month, but after that, the rent and board he paid his parents constituted his biggest monthly outlay, followed by his car's running costs. Next were books, and both live and recorded music. He bought perhaps half a dozen books a year on architecture, maritime history, naval history, and marine engineering, but books, like music recordings, were hugely expensive, for they were all imported from abroad, and he had to exercise enormous self discipline over his spending on these luxuries. During his entire two years working at the store, Alexander bought only eight classical music and opera LPs. But in both 1974 and 1975 he bought season tickets for the opera at the Nico Malan Theatre in Adderley Street.

Alexander immensely enjoyed these performances of grand opera, attending a performance of each of the operas staged during the year. The atmosphere at the opera in the evenings had a fairy tale quality about it, Alexander thought. Some of the opera-goers wore evening dress, their costumes set off by the enormous, dramatic foyer, whose walls, sheathed in glowing honey coloured marble, reflected the scores of lights in the chandeliers which lit up the vast space. The grand staircase intensified the drama of the foyer. These visual effects thrilled Alexander, as did the sound of the orchestra tuning up in the pit, and he felt an exquisite sense of anticipation and excitement as the lights were dimmed in the auditorium, and the musicians all came together on the same note, and then the opening chords of the overture were heard as the stage curtains were drawn back.

Alexander had few but the most casual social exchanges with his fellows. Had it not been for his regular attendance at Holy Communion on Sunday mornings at the Anglican congregation of Christ Church in Constantia, and his occasional presence at evensong during the week, Alexander would rarely have spoken to anyone outside of work and his family. Only twice did he take a young woman on the store's staff to the opera. In neither case did he find these young women had very much in common with him. His passions were too singular to find them shared by either of them. Once, however, his Aunt Margaret accompanied him to the opera, and Alexander was proud to be seen with her by his side. She was, he thought, a very beautiful woman, tall and slim, with a long face and high cheekbones, and a long, narrow nose. She wore a dress of dove grey silk, and a triple strand necklace of silver and jet which had belonged to Alexander's grandmother. Alexander was wearing his best suit, of charcoal wool with a faint pinstripe.

'You're looking really lovely, Aunt Margaret,' he had said, when he collected her at Hohenstein, where the Boyd family had stayed on after Aunt Mary's death. Aunt Margaret ran the hotel and she had become a surrogate mother to his cousins James and Tom.

'Thank you, Sandy. You're looking very smart too,' Aunt Margaret had replied. 'It's nice having a grown up nephew to take me to the opera. Your uncle would never do so.'

For his twentieth birthday in 1975, his Aunt Margaret had bought him the latest edition of *Kobbé's Opera Book*. This was a huge, weighty volume, as substantial as a medieval Bible, and Alexander could now read up on the opera he would be seeing, and study its libretto with English translation, if he wished.

Alexander got along easily enough with his fellow trainee managers (for although Alexander was one of the few of these youngsters who was now a manager himself, he still attended lectures with them several times a week). There was a scattering of other co-workers whom he routinely engaged in somewhat superficial conversation, but he made only one real friend during his time at the store. This was Richard, the young man with whom he sometimes hiked in the mountains, and with whom he would, in the European summer of 1976, travel through France to Pamplona in northern Spain for the *Fiesta de San Fermìn* (popularised by Ernest Hemingway in his 1926 novel *The Sun Also Rises*, and known around the world for its daily bull run).

Alexander was a competent department manager and buyer, but he had not yet learned how to be a social creature. There were times when he felt lonely; when he wished he still had a truly close friend like Philip, his friend during high school days, had been. For the most part however, Alexander did not miss the company of others. His pursuits – whether hiking, or reading, or listening to music – did not require the company of others to enjoy. He had his family at home to love him, and his relations on the Peninsula to visit. Alexander's cousins James and Tom had sold Hohenstein to a national hotel chain in 1975. They had bought a house on the side of the hill above Fish Hoek. Aunt Margaret and her family had moved in with them, but during 1977, after James had turned twenty-one, Aunt Margaret and her family had gone to live with her father on the small farm Rory Maclean had bought outside Fish Hoek, three months after his wife, Jeanie, had died. (This farm was to become for a while Alexander's home also in the mid nineteen-eighties, and it would remain his second home, even after Grandpa Rory's death in the late nineteen-eighties, for his Aunt Margaret and her family had continued living at the farm).

Alexander handed in his notice on Friday 28th November, and spent his last day at work on the 31st December, a Wednesday. It was high summer in Cape Town. On the very early morning of Friday 30th January 1976, having said goodbye to his aunt and grandfather a few days earlier, Alexander's family drove him to D. F. Malan Airport. He was far too excited to feel sad at parting from his family for what might be a very long time, but his mother and father both embraced him, which was something he only rarely remembered them having done in the past.

His mother had insisted Alexander accompany her to a photographer's studio in Cape Town earlier that month, where half a dozen black and white portrait photographs of her son were taken. They showed a gentle, long faced young man with clear skin and wide set, slightly amused eyes, on whose full mouth was the hint of a smile. His straight blonde hair was cut in a pageboy bob. Alexander would probably be returning to Cape Town in September, but no one could be quite certain of this. He gave his grandfather a print of one of the studio photographs, and his Aunt Margaret received one also. Aunt Margaret, looking at the photograph said 'You've turned out a handsome young man, Sandy – so much like your father at the same age.'

At D. F. Malan Airport, dry eyed, Alexander caught the dawn flight for Johannesburg, where he would connect with the day long flight for London, with one refuelling stop at Las Palmas in the Canaries. Within a minute of take off from D. F. Malan, Alexander could see the cobalt blue waters of False Bay below him, the surface of the sea flecked with white horses which were tinged with pink as they caught the sun, which had barely broken above the horizon as it rose in the east. The aircraft banked to port, and climbing rapidly, it flew above the Hottentots Holland range and over the mountains beyond, heading north-east for Johannesburg. They were soon too high for Alexander to make out any details far below, not that there would have been much to see, for before long they had left the folds and creases of the mountain ranges behind, and were flying over the Great Karoo.

Living and working in London, travelling slowly through France in midsummer with Richard, his friend from Cape Town, and working in the Scottish West Highlands later that summer, all contributed towards gains in Alexander's self confidence, and as a result, he became a far more social creature. He learned to rely much more on the help and well disposed regard of others, and he discovered a surprising talent for making friends. As a consequence of flattering attentions paid him by a number of people, Alexander became rather more conscious of his own good looks during this period, and this new found self awareness further boosted his self confidence. He was tall, and although still very slim, he was no longer desperately thin. His height, his head of thick red-gold hair (which he had had cut short soon after arriving in London), and his well formed, expressive features, leant him a striking appearance. He began to understand that people might find him quite attractive. How strange, he sometimes thought, that there had been so little evidence of this at school. Alexander did not yet appreciate that people are drawn to self confidence. He had possessed little self confidence during his high school years, but a great deal of that compelling quality clung to him now, just a few years later. Alexander sloughed off the last vestiges of the crippling self consciousness that had blighted his later high school years and his year at university, and which had lingered on during his two years working in Cape Town.

A girl named Màiri, who worked with Alexander at the hotel in Oban, on Scotland's west coast, played a large part in Alexander's deciding that he was, after all, loveable. Not only was Alexander (who had never before had a girlfriend) strongly attracted to her, but astonishingly, she seemed to feel the same way about him. Màiri, with her hair as dark and shining as jet, and her flawless complexion the colour of new ivory, had eyes of the deepest blue, whose shade, Alexander decided, was that of the ocean. In her person was exhibited, Alexander believed, a Celtic genetic strain predating the Norse invasions, predating even the arrival of the Irish occupiers who had given their name to the country that had become, in time, Scotland. She was from the Hebridean island of Barra, and a majority of the islanders still spoke Gaelic. Alexander was as much drawn to the romance represented in Màiri's person, as to the rather lovely girl herself.

The summer of seventy-six in the British Isles would long be remembered as an exceptionally warm, dry one. At about

ten o'clock in the morning, after the breakfast rush (for both
Alexander and Màiri waited on tables in the hotel), she and
Alexander would cross the road and lean over the harbour
railings, seeing a bewildering array of boats – not only brightly
painted fishing boats, but ferries of all sizes and shapes, as well as
a variety of pleasure yachts and motor cruisers – tied up against
the quay, or moored on the water. Often the sun shone down,
and after a while the two young people would find a bench and
sit and gaze across the water (whose shining blue was almost the
colour of Màiri's eyes, Alexander thought) towards the distant
hills of Mull, where Alexander's paternal grandparents had been
born. This morning, towards the end of August, Alexander felt
himself possessed of a sudden *tristesse*. He took Màiri's hand and
looking at her he said 'My summer here will end, and I will go
across the seas again, and I will think of you, here, for this is a
fairy land.'

'Oh, *mo ghràidh*, it is the *seanchaidh* I hear in you. But so sad!'
Alexander laughed. 'It is the Islander in me, Màiri.'

Alexander, aged twenty-one, was still an innocent. He had
never done more than kiss Màiri, and this he did now, as they
sat in the sun, with the loom of the islands lying far off across the
waters. A big Caledonian MacBrayne ferry from the Outer Isles,
the first of the day, was growing rapidly larger as it drew nearer,
then it slowed, and as it approached the quayside, the bows began
to open, like the jaws of some great beast.

'I shall come back one day,' Alexander said.

'Can you ever return to the land of the fairies?' Màiri asked.

'Oh – I think I shall.'

And forty years later, after a life full of incident, heartache and
passing joys, Alexander came to live in the West Highlands.

But if you would know all that happened to Alexander during
those forty years, then you must next read *Hemispheres: the Life of
Alexander Maclean*, to be published later.

"The childhood shows the man, as morning shows the day," wrote John Milton, in Paradise Regained. *Alexander's restless and questing spirit as an adult was already evident when, aged twelve, he had set off from home on long solo bike rides to Rondebosch town centre, and sometimes beyond, to Newlands Forest. So too that other side of his nature, the gentleness and sensitivity he had possessed as a boy, was never to be lost. By the time Alexander reached the gateway to old age, his character was recognisably that of the boy he had been fifty years earlier. And he thanked God for this, for that boy had not been undeserving of love.*

Robert Dewar, Lochaber, August 2021.